for my father

MEET ME
AT THE
RASCAL

HARRY
MILLER

Sagging
Meniscus

Set in Williams Caslon Text with LaTeX.

ISBN: 978-1-952386-84-8 (paperback)
ISBN: 978-1-952386-85-5 (ebook)
Library of Congress Control Number: 2023949164

Sagging Meniscus Press
Montclair, New Jersey
saggingmeniscus.com

Formerly, only a few men wrote valuable books. Now, anybody writes and prints anything he likes and poisons people's minds.

—*Mohandas K. Gandhi*

Contents

MEET ME AT THE RASCAL

N THE WANING YEARS of the American republic, there lived a man known to history as The Ambassador, for an office he died before filling. Talk about triumph and tragedy! No sooner was the appellation printed on the distinguished man's business card than it was carved on his headstone. Perhaps the latter medium was, after all, the best place to display such a portentous designation as "The Ambassador." As was then true of so many things, the title conveyed stature without the burdens of responsibility. "Ambassador Ronald A. Schloss" epitomized the exalted mediocrity of his age. Yea, verily:

> *Titles of honor are like the impressions on coins, which add no value to gold or silver, but only render brass current.*

—Laurence Sterne

Alas, we digress. Ronald Schloss was a native of Baltimore, Maryland and graduated from Wesleyan University in 1992. The early nineties were an inauspicious time for young Schloss to emerge from college and enter the job market, owing to the prevailing recession; yet he persevered. Finding no use for his BA in Applied Ni-hilism, he fell back upon his computer savvy and was able to make a decent living as a freelance technical consultant, for businesses large and small, on the eve of the internet age. Taking stock of this success, he followed through. While still in his early twenties, he founded the after-school tutoring chain Lesson Plan, which grew into a massive online learning platform, making him a billionaire.

Entrepreneurial acumen, however, embarrassed him, for it clashed with the flaccid ideals of his education. Having enriched himself as a private individual by offering American families what they wanted, it seemed natural that he should "give back" (or give more?) by assuming public functions as well. Therefore, just as Schloss was poised to take center stage in the new economy, he di-verted his attention to Washington. Appointed to the United States Department of Education, where he rose through the ranks at the Office of Educational Technology, he was, after over a decade as its director, tapped to serve as ambassador to Scotland; but he died before assuming the latter post. More was the pity, because the chameleon quality requisite to survival as a bureaucrat would have equipped him equally well for diplomacy. His passing was greatly lamented. Despite his rapid rise and long career, he'd made no ene-mies. Upon his death, to commemorate his years of service in ED, the agency's main office building in DC, which had been named for LBJ, was rechristened in his honor. Flags flew at half-staff over all government buildings. It was a fitting tribute from the establishment he'd served so faithfully.

Ambassador Schloss resembled Pablo Picasso in one important respect suggested by the singer-songwriter Jonathan Richman.

While he lived, "Ronnie" Schloss was easygoing, generous, yielding—and a bit naïve. All of these traits, even the last one, Schloss had cultivated deliberately, to avoid at all costs becoming what he always posited as the ultimate negative character type: the asshole. In spite of his basic liberality—and of his frequent invocation of "diversity" in his educational work—he regarded his own approach to life as the most *sensible* (God forbid that he should call it "normal") and never considered that others might deviate from it. He believed, in other words, that everyone would always act as he himself did and that everyone's motives, furthermore, were just as benevolent and unselfish as his own. As he always strove to do good, he always assumed the good in others. Nothing made him happier— or more complacent—than being joined in a good cause. The good pursued by others, however, was more nakedly self-serving than the good pursued by him, a distinction he failed to grasp, and thus he became vulnerable to false friends. People whom he took to be in the same boat with him were often pulling with their oars in different directions. There were many who found it both convenient and profitable to associate with him. They counterfeited his decency to obtain, and exploit, not only his trust but that of any would-be watchdog. Some of these opportunists were to be found among his copious minions. Some of them, as we shall see, were of his own house. Consequently, though he himself stood out as an island of probity, he was surrounded, as it were, by an archipelago of volcanic wantonness. Many times the spewing ash threatened to enshroud even him. Not once, however, did The Ambassador apprehend the slightest danger. To guard himself against those closest to him was alien to his nature.

His wife, Bonnie Juckman, was a terror. Like many women of her epoch, she demanded to be taken seriously, but the means by which she enforced this demand—preemptive aggression against everyone with whom she had dealings—was exceptional. If she never terrorized her husband, it was because she didn't need to. His submission preempted her aggression. The daughter of a Pikesville property developer, she had always been extraordinarily tall and had loomed over Ronnie from kindergarten through graduation at Baltimore's premier purveyor of precociousness (and Wesleyan warm-up act): the Park School in bucolic Brooklandville. Even as they were immersed in the school's progressive pedagogy, they embodied the most primitive hierarchy. The couple looked like a Valkyrie walking a dog. The dog needed no leash but clung to his master, through their years at Park, Wesleyan, and beyond.

The Ambassador had at a young age married into her family. Uxorilinear unions were then enjoying a renewed popularity. The arrangement suited his amenable personality while conforming to the fashionable theory that if America was to become kinder and gentler, the most fortunate Americans would have to wean themselves from privilege, to cease insisting on having things their way. For Ronnie Schloss, an unconditional surrender of a marriage would satisfy the historical moment's requirement of eschewing advantage and embracing disempowerment. A proud Wesleyan man (the phrase is ironic), he desired not only his wife but "her" children (meaning their children) to retain the Juckman surname. It was a victory over patriarchy. He would have become a Juckman himself, but Lesson Plan was then taking off, and Bonnie decreed that its CEO should avoid such a confusing relabeling. He knew she was right, of course, and so he remained Ronnie Schloss for her sake.

His indulgence of her was habitual. It comforted him. The imperative of gender reversal aside, Ronnie Schloss's inborn pliability led him always to defer to anyone who seemed to know what she was doing. Since Bonnie so insistently knew what she was doing, Ronnie felt in good hands. From the planning of his wardrobe, to the styling of his hair, he left his wife in charge. *Well, why not let her handle the little things?* he rationalized. The minutiae of office organization, too, he soon ceded to her, leaving him, he supposed, free to contemplate the big picture; and "Ms. Bonnie" thus became a fixture, first at Lesson Plan and then in ED.

Ms. Bonnie was The Ambassador's stronger half, if not his better half.

"Ms. Bonnie" had a good memory and diverse other abilities. She honed these advantages constantly. Since childhood, she viewed the world as her classroom and every situation as a source of experience, an opportunity to expand her repertoire of practical skills. Soon, her proficiencies defied any resume to list them. Most of these talents had political uses, and politics, indeed, formed her chief interest and pastime. All other subjects bored her. She was the definition of a political animal. For such a soul as hers, it was an opportune time to be alive. She could recite verbatim almost all of the denunciatory rants of the Clinton and Bush years. They were catnip to her. She collected bumper stickers and managed to acquire "Lyin' King" caricatures of both presidents. She sold handmade "Shoot Hillary First" henleys and "Shoot Cheney First" tie-dyes to grateful Hopkins students. She was especially fond of dissembling press secretaries and enjoyed re-watching the television broadcasts she recorded, showcasing George Stephanopoulos's and Ari Fleischer's finest performances. She was glued to cable talk shows. Not incidentally, she was also a fan of professional wrestling. Such programming wasn't Ronnie's cup of tea, and she tsk-tsked at his ignorance of how the real world worked, thinking *Good thing he has me.*

Even as Ronnie attained eminence in the Department of Education, he could do almost nothing—be it official or family business—without her permission. Soon it began to occur even to him that reliance on Bonnie no longer counted as wise policy, for it had ceased to be policy at all. To be sure, it had always been a good idea to refer matters to the omnicompetent Bonnie, but now the good husband had no choice. He was completely unmanned. What had begun as chivalrous deference had devolved into an abject dependence on wifely favor. No matter how slavish his condition, however, he still considered it proof of his own goodness. How charming he must have seemed to himself, as a latter-day Amadis of Gaul, with Bonnie as his Princess Oriana, "at whose slightest angry word heard by him—for such was his great fear of angering her—he would bury himself alive." Thus did the willfully meek dream of inheriting the Earth. Paralyzed with fear, he read her countenance before committing himself to anything. He was attuned to her most subtle expression. When no sign of her approbation was manifest, his entire thought process shut down. The "I'm with Stupid" T-shirt might as well have been designed for him—or rather for Bonnie. At Martin's Tavern in Georgetown, the head waiter knew to look at Bonnie whenever he asked, "And for you, sir?" (She always ordered him the catch of the day, to keep him from acquiring a favorite entree.) On those rare occasions when Bonnie was not at his side, Ronnie could only put off whatever decision was needed from him. "I'll have to get back to you on that," he always said.

Sometimes, Ms. Bonnie took on government functions in her own name, and no official—federal, state, or local—ever failed to obey her. Evidently, she'd come to expect free rein. She convened educational conferences, recognized meritorious teachers, and approved classroom technology. She awarded grants and promulgated pedagogical guidelines. Her signature was recognized in the White House. She could fire people or get them reassigned to other departments, subject to union rules. Management consultants took notice of the "Bonnie Juckman Method" of organizational control, lauding it as the best means known for compelling "robotic obedience" from any corporation or bureau. They began inviting her to address leadership seminars, and her talks drew huge audiences. On the strength of her formidable reputation, she became notorious as the true tyrant of Baltimore. (Desperate for any sort of notoriety, Baltimore embraced her, tyranny and all.) Together with her amiable ventriloquist dummy of a husband, Bonnie Juckman counted as the most significant political force to emerge from the city since Spiro Agnew. Her obsession with power was paying off. The Juckman family compound on Velvet Valley Way in the suburb of Stevenson was jokingly— and fearfully—referred to as the fourth branch of government. Alternating American flags and Department of Education banners lined the driveway. News networks often broadcast the power couple's announcements from their front porch.

Bonnie and Ronnie bred quite a brood.

Ronnie Schloss and Bonnie Juckman had three sons, of whom the oldest was named Micah, and four daughters, of whom the second was named Marigold. The Juckman young received the best upbringing that money could buy. Naturally, they all attended Park School, where their parents sat on the board of trustees. All seven were petted by their teachers, giving each the outsized ego that such special attention always confers; but in the cases of Micah and Marigold, the spoiling went both ways, for the two children displayed such extraordinary self-assurance that their teachers felt graced by their presence in their classes. It was Micah and Marigold, Bonnie observed, who held the most potential for carrying on the Juckman legacy. The matriarch considered them equally scions, yet she would have done well to note certain differences in disposition. Although both children were indeed gifted and talented enough for the role Bonnie envisaged for them, Micah tended to think of the family as something that served him, while only Marigold viewed it as something she should serve. Understanding of this divergent reality would come too late for all concerned.

Marigold, who went by the name Goldie, was married to a man named Morgan Schwartzenberg, a second-generation lawyer with an ignoble face, whose every movement suggested a profound spiritual instability. How did Goldie end up with such a specimen? The marriage was arranged by Bonnie, who had proved to her own satisfaction that a strong woman could best project her power through a cipher of a husband; yet Goldie often wished that her mother had chosen a more appealing force multiplier than Morgan, for the man was utterly charmless. In fact, he was a philistine. He cared nothing for music or art. (Occasionally, he would give to the BMA or the BSO, just to get his name on the wall of donors, an admirable practice we shall see exemplified below.) He loved only cars and money, and when he spoke of either, he cackled and brayed and convulsed his body. His enthusiasms were measurable by the drool on his shirt. On those rare occasions when Morgan could be confined to a chair, his eyes darted left and right, like those of a rat. What beady peepers they were, one could not help but notice. His table manners, too, were rodential, and indeed the entire routine of his life amounted to one furry blur of nibbling, gnawing, pilfering, and peculating. Such a creature does not marry for love. He viewed his marriage into the Juckman family as a business venture, which of course it was. It was a political arrangement as well. The only difference between his conception of the union and Ms. Bonnie's lay in the portentous question "Who benefits?" It sure wasn't Goldie.

As for Goldie herself, she was a voracious reader and a skilled poet. She published a collection of simple romantic short verse, entitled *Easy Lays*, before graduating from college (Wesleyan, on the legacy plan); meanwhile, her literary intake was of such great volume that dozens of splayed-open hardbacks and paperbacks lay strewn about her desk and bed. Her taste, however, ran toward the modern rather than the classical, a preference which cut her off from received wisdom, even as it afforded her an advantageous familiarity with contemporary culture. This familiarity, at any rate, she put to good use. After a brief stint at a literary agency in New York, she returned to Baltimore and launched her own concern, called Secret Bookshelf, which specialized in YA trans ninja. It was a fortuitous choice of genre. Success came quickly, with the publication of her client KD Condor's blockbuster, *Tommy or Tammy? Either Way, I'm Gonna Cut Your Throat*.

While still a girl, Goldie was happy and content to remain naturally plain. As she grew to womanhood, she became an unrivaled beauty. Her appeal was internal. Though she was always immaculately dressed and made up, it was her inviting smile that left the deepest impression. It conveyed an available loneliness, as though crying out "Complete me." In the society pages of *Baltimore Magazine*, she invariably appeared without her husband. None regretted his absence. Any photographer's attempt to capture such an incongruous couple would have broken his camera.

Goldie and Micah got along very well.

Goldie had always been very companionable with her brother Micah, and some said she indulged him in his willfulness. The siblings brought out the best and the worst in each other—or actually the best in the one and the worst in the other. In contrast to Goldie and Morgan, Goldie and Micah were photographed together quite often, resulting in a gallery of snapshots resembling prom pictures, each showing Goldie resplendent in the profoundest contentment and Micah exuding an impish *self*-satisfaction. Perhaps they represented nothing more than the attraction of opposites in nature. Goldie was a couple of years older and had begun hovering over Micah when he was a toddler. (Bonnie, of course, was too busy hovering over her husband.) She was always the selfless giver and Micah the accustomed receiver. The transactional imbalance suited them both and became ingrained in their daily lives. Well beyond childhood, they continued to eat and even bathe together. (How odd that "hungry" and "dirty" should carry such risqué connotations, for, as these feelings lead one to eat and to bathe, they result in satiety and cleanliness.) To accompany each activity, they sang songs from their father's old record collection, remembered from before adolescence: As they spread cream cheese on each other's bagels at breakfast, they chanted Prince's "Starfish and Coffee"; as they lathered each other's bodies in the shower before bed, they performed the Beatles' "One After 909," modifying one of its lines to "Only fool around, only fool around with me," which they orchestrated in harmony to accentuate an especially sudsy climax. Goldie was a mezzo-soprano, Micah a baritone, although he could summon up a falsetto when the occasion demanded. The siblings' marriages by no means constrained their intimacy, as Micah (with his bride) continued to live, and Goldie maintained her office, at Juckman Manor. Goldie was in no rush to go home to Morgan and often spent the night at Velvet Valley Way. The two-part harmony never stopped; the water bill remained hefty. Goldie and Micah hovered between innocence and guilt, for while neither was ashamed of their relationship before God, both anticipated being shamed, should the sinful world intrude upon their Edenic existence.

When they were discovered in the shower together by Micah's wife, the former Danielle Caplan, it was the husband, Micah, and not the wife who waxed the more indignant. Micah's wrath was proportional to the size of his erection. "Goddammit! Can't a man get a little privacy?" he bellowed, making the great house shake. "Have I ever barged in on *you* in the shower?" Micah exiled Danielle to a guest bedroom. Whatever remained of his connubial sensibility went into exile as well. He texted her his whereabouts, expecting her to keep out of his way. She complied with his wishes and made herself scarce, even as the hope grew in her womb that Micah and Danielle— she could close her eyes and still see their wedding chuppah—would be brought back together; but as far as Micah was concerned, he and Danielle were kaput. He bided his time until she was giving birth to his child and then took the opportunity to poison her to death with arsenic. Micah had extracted the fatal substance (following instructions published on the internet) from ceramic glazes nicked from artist friends. He slipped it into her oxygen mask while the nurses were accompanying her to the bathroom for one final pee before her delivery. Returned to bed, and with the mask pumping the stuff into her nose and mouth, Danielle began hemorrhaging and went into convulsions; the baby didn't survive her. The poison remained undetected until her autopsy. (It was Micah, of course, playing the part of the bereft husband in order to escape suspicion, who demanded the autopsy.) Its discovery elicited but little surprise. Arsenic had shown its toxic face at Velvet Valley Way not long before. Because one of the family maids had just died after showing similar symptoms, Danielle was assumed to have perished as the result of an accidental exposure affecting the whole household. Decontamination crews inspected the mansion and removed traces of arsenic from Micah's wardrobe, thus avoiding further tragedy. The former Ms. Caplan had been Micah's Wesleyan girlfriend and was not a local girl. Meek and mousy and unconnected, she had never been cut out for Juckman life. Her passing went largely unmourned. Baltimore gossips expected Micah to marry better next time. The extent of the family's nonchalance, however, began lending an off-color tinge to its heretofore gleaming reputation.

Ms. Bonnie's younger brother was brought in as overseer.

Adding to the unconventionality of the family was Bonnie Juckman's younger brother Tinus, who was sinister, volatile, and capable of any outrage. "To run any kind of organization," Bonnie informed her leadership seminars, "you need bad people as well as good people," and Tinus was—well, you get it. Tinus regarded himself as the muscle to go with Bonnie's brains. As long as he maintained this conception of their relationship, it was okay with his big sister. It was Bonnie's long sufferance of Tinus's rambunctiousness that inured her to the boorish character of Morgan Schwartzenberg or to the increasing creepiness of her own son Micah. Creeps didn't faze her. In fact, Bonnie Juckman believed she could manage anybody. Her sense of power increased with the coarseness of the company she kept.

Ms. Bonnie began employing Tinus in various family tasks. (His previous job was head football coach for Baltimore's Friends School, which left him unfulfilled. Tinus was overjoyed when Bonnie asked for his help but crestfallen that "Goon" would not be his official job title. "Executive Enforcer" would have to do.) Most of these duties required a combination of accounting skill and personnel management expertise, for Tinus's chief responsibility was to ensure that none of the family's support staff engaged in embezzlement. Performance of this duty required him to do little more than to pace around behind people's desks, sometimes checking figures but mostly just acting intimidating. He would have to content himself, Bonnie explained, with cracking only a metaphorical whip. Content enough he seemed to be.

Before a year had passed, however, he was abusing one of Ambassador Schloss's personal assistants, savagely beating her whenever she resisted his advances. As his advances, and her refusals, were copious, so too were the beatings. The most egregious of these attacks occurred in Bonnie Juckman's *salle de bain*, to which Tinus had ordered his prey to report, to help him aim the bidet. Revolted, the employee, a one-legged foot masseuse named Dolores Nostromo, tried to flee, but Tinus kicked away one of her crutches and she lost her balance, hitting her head on the sink as she fell. When the young woman threatened to go to the police, the Juckmans had no choice but to pay her off. It was not a small settlement. The money spent to ensure her silence should have impressed Tinus with the importance of avoiding scandal, but he went right on bantering in the staff locker room about his adventures Down Under: "B'day, mate!" he crowed. Even a muscle man should have had brains enough to avoid behaving like that. Ms. Bonnie was disgusted and took her brother to court, where he received ten strokes of the bamboo. If Tinus was surprised by the harsh treatment, then he didn't know his sister. The corporal punishment was rendered at Bonnie's insistence, the judge accepting her argument that the super-rich could shrug off any standard (or super-standard) financial settlement. Never mind that the plaintiff was plenty rich herself. Every once in a while, Bonnie reasoned, people needed to be taught a lesson; their wounds, both physical and emotional, would heal before too long. Discipline needed to be maintained. Her little brother was a willing guard dog anyway, and a few days in the doghouse would if anything add to his serviceability. Of course, Ms. Bonnie was right. Tinus Juckman fell in and out of his family's graces many times, in this general way. Periodically growing too big for his britches, he often provoked Bonnie's chastisement. He always came scuffling back. After all, he couldn't go back to coaching football at Friends. On this particular occasion, in fact, he was permitted to recuperate in the main house. Bonnie herself applied the aloe to his welts. Soon he was pacing the grounds and shaking the trees as though nothing had happened.

It was time for the paterfamilias to pass the baton.

The Ambassador died in 2026. He was, as we have already related, at the height of his career. He departed life unexpectedly, without the prolonged, thoughtful decline or the accompaniment of whirring hospital machinery he'd always imagined to be his due. No chance was afforded him to impart any words of wisdom to his progeny.

His death was front-page news nationwide, and Baltimore fell into a state of shock. Schools were closed. The former Senator Theater, just renamed The Ambassador, was draped in black crepe in his honor. Amid the tears, however, there was also puzzlement. As he had always been healthy and strong, there were many who found his sudden passing rather odd. Any power family would have received attention under such circumstances, but The Ambassador's house attracted special scrutiny. The incipient fishiness of the Juckmans' reputation had by now grown potent enough to fertilize a fine crop of rumor. Probing questions were asked privately and in the media. Though The Ambassador's reputation was sterling, the same could not be said about his family and associates, and conspiracy theorists began to speculate that he'd become involved in one of their shenanigans. Gossips rubbed their hands. "The sins of the father," they began to pontificate, "no, wait, not the father; everyone *but* the father is crooked." Cable and internet pundits, the kind Bonnie followed so fervently, wondered aloud about what pile of sleaze The Ambassador had stepped in.

Their suspicions were reinforced by the fact that a cousin of his in Severna Park, Arnold Kiester, had recently been defrauded and had taken his malefactor to court. Kiester was a likely enough victim. It seemed like an open and shut case. As routine as it seemed to be, though, it shed unflattering light on the type of "shenanigans" that were now assumed to have occupied The Ambassador's circle. Kiester alleged that he'd been bilked in a student loan consolidation scheme. The loans totaled half a million dollars and had been taken out on behalf of Kiester's son—for him to attend Wesleyan, as a matter of fact. He produced bank records showing two years of monthly payments to the consolidator, who had never paid off the original creditor. This kind of thing happened all the time, and it was not hard to imagine it happening to Arnold Kiester.

However, the accused, an insurance broker named Harvey Karp, tallying all the plunder he'd amassed, found it within his means to bribe the judge, and thus he filed a false counter-accusation against Kiester, for which Kiester would, Karp expected, be condemned to death. Karp was hoping for a public beheading. (College education had become a big deal, in the course of America's decline. See our discussion of the proliferation of "education crimes" below.) Specifically, Karp placed Kiester at the center of a human trafficking ring, disguised as a study-abroad consultancy. The countercharge represented a significant upping of the ante, in keeping with Karp's desire for blood. It was Kiester, Karp alleged, and not himself who had taken advantage of young people's thirst for knowledge, enticing dozens of victims from overseas to enroll for a semester at an American campus, only to snatch their passports and indenture them as hotel maids, country club groundskeepers, or worse. Alas, this kind of thing happened all the time, too, and it was not hard to imagine Arnold Kiester making it happen.

The judge, however, knew that Kiester was a relative of the recently-named Ambassador, and so he dithered. Here, the judge, the Honorable Solomon Sullivan of the Anne Arundel County Circuit Court, was playing the part of prudence. As long as an important person was in the game, it behooved him to wait and see which way the chips were likely to fall. He certainly didn't want to bet on the wrong number. Putting off his decision was in any case profitable, for the impatient Karp began showering him with more money. The amounts Karp advanced totaled more than Kiester's original loan. Thus was the judge content to let Karp twist in the wind for a while longer. Time was money for Judge Sullivan.

Sensing an opening, Kiester urged his illustrious cousin to write to the judge on his behalf, and Ambassador Schloss did in fact compose a letter that would surely have straightened everything out. It suited the ever-helpful Ambassador to ride to the rescue, especially if it meant lending his name. References, testimonials, vouchers— these were the hallmarks of civilization, the bases of an orderly society. It never occurred to The Ambassador that unscrupulous people might try to profit from his name, and he continued to lend it to whomever asked for it. There was no better character witness than Ronnie Schloss, and if he said that Arnold Kiester was a good man, then you could bet your kiester that Arnold Kiester was a good man. It was a pleasant thought. The Ambassador clicked "Print," and that should have been the end of it. He hummed as he licked and sealed the envelope.

At this juncture, though, Karp advanced a bribe of five hundred thousand dollars to Goldie Juckman, and Goldie brought the matter to the attention of her mother. Here was a bit of family business requiring a top-level decision. The reason Karp went through Goldie was because it was easier to track her down at her literary agency than it was to approach the powerful Ms. Bonnie. (Of course, tracking down a literary agent doesn't mean getting a reply, but such a vast sum of money could not fail to get Goldie's attention.)

"A nice guy is one thing," the matriarch said, "but half a million bucks is . . ."

"Nothing to sneeze at," offered Goldie. It wasn't even a close call.

Action was of the essence. Ms. Bonnie quickly gave orders that her husband's letter be intercepted, and then the two women proceeded to alter its contents. (The Ambassador had selected a trusted courier to hand-deliver his reference letter, but the man's girlfriend was Bonnie's manicurist, and she alerted Bonnie to her beau's mission just as she and Goldie were discussing Karp's offer.) As they collaborated, they bonded. Mother and daughter had worked together before but never on something so intricate. Both Goldie's way with words and Bonnie's political savvy stood them in good stead. "I see that we didn't send you to Wesleyan for nothing," Bonnie remarked, as Goldie applied the finishing touches to an especially subtle insinuation. Their joint effort was a masterful blending of eloquence and strategy. Forging The Ambassador's letterhead and signature, the Juckman women smiled at a job well done.

According to their rephrasing, Ambassador Schloss admitted that he employed Arnold Kiester as a consultant, but he expressed regret that his cousin's conduct left much to be desired. Years-long familiarity afforded some unflattering observation. The problem was one of character. Simply put, Arnold Kiester was a moving picture of avarice in action. "It's not just my cousin's greedy nature," the complaint went, "but his ability to exploit every opportunity that is so troubling. Such an acquisitive approach to life I have never elsewhere beheld. His eye is always on the main chance. The simplest situation is for him a potential source of profit." In fact (the counterfeit letter continued), Kiester would often wield The Ambassador's authority to oppress and plunder people. "How many he has mulcted in my name I cannot say." This tendency was so concerning, because the reputation so carefully cultivated by The Ambassador over the years—here Goldie inserted the triple invocation of reputation made by Cassio in *Othello*, which she recalled from a manga version and not from the original—could be sullied in an instant by someone like Kiester. On numerous occasions, The Ambassador tried to bring Kiester to heel, to no avail. He ignored Schloss's pleas to desist. "He is not content to quit while he is ahead." Nay, his genius for extortion seemed continually to require greater challenges. He was insatiable. Thus the recent allegation that Kiester had accused a law-abiding man of fraud was not at all surprising. "The only mystery is why something of this sort has not happened sooner. It conforms perfectly to his *modus operandi*," the new letter read. (Goldie thought a little Latin would lend the indictment an authoritative air.) Human trafficking, furthermore, was not beyond him. "He might as well have kidnapped the students himself." It was merely the logical extension of Kiester's love of exploiting people for money.

The forged letter urged that Kiester receive the maximum punishment, else there would be no end to his villainy. "Moral suasion would be lost on him. He possesses no morality to which one might appeal. No form of mercy will induce him to mend his ways." Lethal injection was too good for him. Why spare him any pain, who had caused so much of it? No, The Ambassador's ghost writers concluded, the wretch Kiester needed to be made an example, the grimmer the better.

True, the wording was a bit over the top, and hyperbole—not to mention cruelty—was most unlike The Ambassador, which strongly suggested that others were involved in the missive's drafting; but it wouldn't have mattered, even if editorial assistance could have been proven. The judge, receiving the letter, suspected nothing about it, for it was commonly known that Ambassador Schloss's correspondence was often drafted by Ms. Bonnie and that Ms. Bonnie's correspondence was often drafted by Goldie. (No one wrote his own correspondence anymore, for Pete's sake.) Anything written over The Ambassador's signature would have proven decisive anyway—just as both Kiester and The Ambassador himself had assumed—and if the Juckman ladies had lent a hand to the endeavor, then the judge was all the happier to receive it with the greatest respect and credence; besides, Bonnie and Goldie were The Ambassador's flesh and blood and surely as upright as he. And so, Bonnie and Goldie ended up making the decisive play. Their forged testimony won the day for Karp. Never was half a million better spent. As he had calculated, criminal charges against Kiester proceeded from the civil case, and The Ambassador's hijacked testimony settled the outcome of the trial. For one final time, the good man's name was leveraged by a paskudnyak.

Accordingly, Arnold Kiester was flogged to death. There was no saving him. His lawyers didn't even bother to appeal, for they would have been confronted with The Ambassador's fatal letterhead wherever they went. So greased, the wheels of justice turned inexorably and quickly. The sentence was carried out on State Circle in Annapolis, in conformity with DOJ guidelines mandating public executions for heinous crimes such as human trafficking. DOJ knew the mood of the people—eager for government to "get things done"—and its directives met with little resistance. Bureaucrats were on hand to compute a new Policy Effectiveness Metric—a ratio of capital punishments per human trafficking cases—in the hope that it would go up and so prove to voters that the Department was on the ball. Ambassador Schloss, assuming that his intervention on behalf of Kiester had secured the latter's release, knew nothing of the reversal until a driver in his employ reported to have seen the condemned man on the day of his death, tattered and bleeding. It was a still morning in Annapolis, with storm clouds churning above. The driver, Pharaoh Goldfarb, had just exited a neighborhood delicatessen with a carry-out crab cake, when he chanced to look up at the scaffold across the street. By coincidence, the State Flogger was eating a crab cake on his breakfast break between onslaughts, while Kiester waited. (Of course, had the execution occurred some five years later, it would have been televised. What better way to make executions public? The Justice Channel had yet to be greenlighted by the FCC, however, and ratings boards were reluctant to approve the content for general broadcasting, despite bipartisan support for "community-building rituals" such as public executions.) Back in the office, Goldfarb was asked by The Ambassador why he wasn't eating his crab cake, and so he told his boss the bad news. At this intelligence, Ambassador Schloss bewailed his cousin's fate. (Bonnie had kept her husband in the dark about the case, of course, hence his surprise.) Hurrying to his study, he located the original computer file. It was named ArnieFavor.doc. He read over the sterling character assessment he'd given Kiester. "Consummately upright" . . . "a pillar of the Severna Park healthcare consultancy" . . . "too much of a nebbish to break the law"—every phrase was as much of a gem as he remembered. The screen seemed to go blurry with his bewilderment. "Arnie dead? But I wrote such a nice letter for him!" he swore. Goldfarb had never seen the old man in a state of such agitation. "In the old days, an ambassador's word meant something!" Schloss pounded on his desk, sending a wave of vibration through his Ten Emperors of the Qing Dynasty bobblehead collection, which nodded *en masse* in fervent agreement. The gentle patriarch was making an uncharacteristic fuss. "Shittypiss! If I didn't know any better," he spouted to anyone who would listen, "I'd say there's something wacky about the Kiester case." He started making phone calls, as he raged. Ms. Bonnie and Goldie were discomfited at his protestations, but not for long, for Ambassador Schloss suddenly breathed his last. Bonnie came in to calm him down, advising him to keep to his daily routine and leave everything to her, and so reassured, he resumed his accustomed placidity. He went quietly during his afternoon nap, on the couch in the study. A downloaded but unopened issue of *The New Yorker* glowed forlornly from the e-reader on the floor next to him. The medical examiner checked for arsenic, but none was found, for Bonnie had poisoned him with an uncommon radioactive isotope. The lethal nuclide was her pacifier of last resort, kept in readiness in a cosmetics case. She'd dropped it into the chamomile tea he always enjoyed before stretching out. The stuff worked, it was said, like slowly-rising temperature on a frog; The Ambassador felt nothing as his blood boiled and his DNA denatured.

The messenger who had been charged with delivering The Ambassador's original letter to the judge, and who had brought it instead to Ms. Bonnie and Goldie, soon died as well. The same isotope was used. A cup of coffee in the staff room did the trick for him. Bonnie would have to find her manicurist a new companion. Ambulances became a common sight on Velvet Valley Way. (There were actually only two more ambulance sorties than usual that month, for the Juckmans, having some influence with the University of Maryland Health System, often used them to ride to routine doctor's appointments.) Ms. Bonnie, however, ordered the drivers to silence their sirens. Nonetheless, speculation continued. The affair was soon the talk of the town, and everyone believed Bonnie and Goldie Juckman to be behind The Ambassador's death. Insinuations about the Juckman women followed the pattern of political pornography that had long titillated Bonnie, so it was a matter of some poetic justice that she was now on the receiving end of it. Suspicion was unwarranted in the case of poor Goldie, who felt guilty enough for having helped to create the stressful situation that overtaxed her father's nerves but who would never have done anything to harm him; yet both Juckman ladies received dirty looks. The pointed whisperings about Bonnie and Goldie surrounded even The Ambassador's funeral. No one, however, would dare accuse them in public. Soon the controversy ran itself out, and the Juckman stock held steady. Time marched on.

The materfamilias stepped up and ran into unexpected trouble.

With her husband gone, Ms. Bonnie became if anything even bolder. If she did pause to mourn for The Ambassador, it was only for an instant. Never the sort to brood, she explained to well-wishers that immersion in work would best help her to cope, especially if it was the kind of work she'd often performed in The Ambassador's shadow. Assuming direct command would be therapeutic, and she was eager to get started. Finally, she could run the family in her own right. Bonnie had less of a need than Ronnie to project an image of stability. Building on The Ambassador's legacy meant expanding into areas he'd never considered, such as education insurance and genome-based learning. The possibilities seemed endless.

At this point, however, Micah Juckman began maneuvering against her, and they became bitter enemies. Apparently, others beside Bonnie had been waiting for their turn in the captain's chair. Bonnie was blindsided. She never anticipated that her claim to leadership would be contested, least of all by her hedonistic son. Though young Juckman had never shown much keenness for intrigue before, he now displayed considerable talent for it. Whereas Bonnie had functioned as a careful and calculating manipulator, improving her skills over years of marriage, Micah was more of an insurgent or saboteur, with an inborn—or perhaps a child's— knack for fucking things up. As for his motivation, it was a simple desire for importance, amplified by a sense of entitlement; but in any case, he was not the kind of person to do anything by halves. In that sense only did he resemble Bonnie.

Micah enticed his mother's younger brother Tinus into his entourage. He feigned a conspiratorial friendship. "Mom's got you on a pretty tight leash, hasn't she?" Micah hissed in his uncle's ear. "I don't know why she's so afraid to turn you loose and see what you can really do for the family." The tactic was designed not only to deprive the matriarch of an ally but also to hurt her. Psychological combat was turning out to be his forte. It was war, in his mind, and he strove not only for his own advantage but for his enemy's ruin. Tinus soon took his leave from Velvet Valley Way, after subjecting Bonnie to a few maledictions suggested by his crafty nephew. Ms. Bonnie swore vengeance, in spite of efforts on the part of family friends to maintain the peace. Micah had hit her in a sore spot, challenging her authority on more than one front. Soon, she too became less interested in common benefit than in vanquishing the foe. Just as Micah had hoped, Bonnie was sinking to his level. In truth, there was not much she could do, for Micah's morbid sense of independence rendered him emotionally invulnerable. He was affronted by the very idea of the happy family, deeming it a cliché, and disaffection became for him an end it itself. The more she threatened him, the more he enjoyed it. It was a case of domestic sadomasochism. The problem was that Micah, an eldest son now bereft of his father, suffered from loneliness. No matter how many people surrounded him at any given time, he assumed their friendship to be factitious or insufficient and that he was alone. Loneliness is a form of hurt, and those who feel hurt can often think of nothing else but hurting others.

With the only intimacy he had ever known now out of reach, Micah became even more dissipated.

He would have turned to his sister Goldie for solace, but she seemed so fixed in his mother's camp that he could no longer trust her, and so he sought substitutes. It was an unhappy expedient. The strategy *seemed* to make sense, for ersatz sympathy was all around him. It was indeed the kind of phoniness that exacerbated Micah's sense of isolation, but at least he was used to it. A pampered youth, he was attended by a veritable harem of boys and girls, and his powers of concentration were such that he could play video games even while enjoying their company. In fact, he'd become adept at handling a PlayStation 27 controller with his right hand while plunging his left down the pants of player two. *Give these whippersnappers enough thumb action*, Micah mused, *and they'll do whatever you want.* Now, though, it just made him miss Goldie.

Micah had moved downtown to Federal Hill after the death of his father, and his well-appointed townhouse, with its rooftop jacuzzi, became a notorious fleshpot. Casa Micah, it was called. Beer kegs and party drugs were as ubiquitous as Xboxes and PlayStations. Micah was the host with the most. At any time of day or night, he could be seen arm in arm with his hangers-on, sharing numerous women between them. They produced as much porn as they consumed, displaying it on floor-to-ceiling TV screens, when they were not being used for Halo 15. Alexa adjusted the tuneage according to the mood. The volume was usually rather high. The police were more likely to join than to break up the orgies. Officers begged to be assigned to his block. Neighbors moved away, and Micah scooped up their properties, incorporating them into his pleasure palace. *The Baltimore Sun* coined a term for this phenomenon, calling it "Babylonian gentrification."

Tinus Juckman, presuming upon some avuncular prerogative, craved an invitation to these revelries, but Micah, now having second thoughts about his uncle's company, offered none, reasoning that, although no one took him (Micah) seriously, at least people could relax with him; but they would never be able to maintain their current level of candor were Uncle Tinus to crash the party. The thought of his doing so was most unappetizing. Micah was already the oldest person at his saturnalias, and he wanted no second satyr. Besides, by dissing Bonnie, Tinus had already served his purpose. It had been gratifying to alienate *someone* from his mother (though not the one he wanted), but having notched the victory, it lost meaning, and he clung ever more firmly to his dissolution. He could keep fucking things up at his leisure, but for now the key word was *leisure*. "Living well is the best revenge," Micah remembered from a bumper sticker he once saw. Presently, however, Tinus stopped waiting for invitations and began showing up unannounced. Anxious to continue his depravities undisturbed, Micah grew once again murderous, resolving to kill Tinus as soon as possible. Readers will note that this was not the first time that Micah had contemplated the taking of human life, for a trespass upon his enjoyment. "Maybe I should poison him. Arsenic might be a bad idea, but I can try something else. That would give Mom a taste of her own medicine," he grumbled. He was only assuming that Ms. Bonnie had poisoned The Ambassador, projecting the evil of his past and planned deeds onto his mother. Micah knew nothing of the isotope in his dad's chamomile, but in his rage he made a lucky guess. In the event, Tinus saved his own life by realizing how unwelcome he was at Casa Micah and leaving the kids to their frolicking.

Goldie Juckman, despite her usual sympathy for her brother, nonetheless remained loyal to her mother. It was Bonnie, after all, who put food on the table, whereas Micah had only put semen on her chest; yet she loved them both. She was really quite torn. Someone of her warm disposition could not fail to be. She texted Micah constantly, but he ignored her, assuming that she was merely acting as Bonnie's messenger. The idea galled him. Here Micah was selling his sister short, for he should have recognized her pure heart and good intentions. (Alas, the son was most unlike the father in this regard, for Micah saw nowhere the goodness that The Ambassador saw everywhere.) She hoped to do well by them both and to effect a reconciliation. Even so, she was acting not at all as Bonnie's agent. Goldie was motivated by personal considerations as well as by family ones. She couldn't fail to see how wounded Bonnie had been by Micah's conduct, and she wanted to patch everything up and thus salve the wound, but in the final analysis she was putting her own feelings first. The truth was that Goldie missed Micah as much as he missed her; given their mutual longing, there was still a chance that both siblings could overcome the unfavorable situation and restore their intimate bond. Closing her eyes, she could see Micah walking in through the door, scruffy but with the old puckish grin on his face. It would have been such a happy reunion. Maybe one of her lovesome text messages would soon have been able to bring it about. Just then, however, came the affair of Rudy Rutowitz, which would make things even more complicated. It was almost as though the ghost of Mr. Murphy, famed for his vexatious Law, conjured up the Rutowitz affair as a horrible prank, designed to inflict as much turmoil as possible. Affairs usually do. Affairs involving a Rutowitz almost always do. In fact, the Rutowitz episode would scotch the last hope that the Juckman family would find peace.

Who was Rudy Rutowitz?

The man was quite insignificant, for all the damage he would do. Given his profession, in fact, he'd been inflicting great damage from the beginning. Rudy Rutowitz had been the late Ambassador' interior decorator. He had come to the Juckmans right on schedule, just as they began to get rich and were eager to transform their cash into social capital through the medium of decorative art. He continued to serve the family after The Ambassador's passing. On each of his ongoing visits to Velvet Valley Way, he took pleasure in noting how abundantly he had left his mark. It was he who had transformed the Juckman mansion into the post-modern nightmare it was, with its forbidding chrome surfaces, inhuman cubist furniture, nauseating oil painting, and monstrous sculpture. Rudy Rutowitz had put Juckman Manor on greater Baltimore's hot list of *première maisons des arrivistes*. The giant stainless-steel dragonfly larva in the fountain court was justly considered his masterpiece. He called it *Tina*.

At this time, Bonnie Juckman's business interests were suffering, owing to her poor relations with Micah. Her son's spiteful behavior had already caused much disruption. The prevailing instability led to the continual postponement of all the new projects she envisioned. The resulting loss of revenue was significant. Having a renegade son not only disconcerted the family's wealth management strategy but also crippled morale. Family strife spelled trouble for the family business, not just because Micah was the presumptive heir to the Juckman empire. Bonnie soon realized that more than the future was at stake. Meltdown threatened in the here and now. In fact, she was concerned that her authority was no longer respected, even in her own household. The leadership expert was facing a crisis of leadership. What's a mover and a shaker to do, if she can't move and shake her own people? Micah's fractiousness was raising the specter of mass mutiny. If an employee grew tired of her strictness, he could happily defect to Micah's establishment, where there was always room for one more in the hot-tub. A few of her younger employees had already walked. Ms. Bonnie felt a keen sympathy for the builders of the Berlin Wall. Discipline de corps, rather than esprit de corps, became her watchword.

One day, therefore, she established a family secretariat in the main hall of the Juckman family compound. Superior management would have to carry the day. Desks were pushed together to accommodate various departments, to oversee Lesson Plan's private business and government contracts, maintain important political and media relationships, and keep tabs on Micah. Additional personnel were hired, in many cases non-Baltimoreans (or even foreigners) fresh out of business school, with no other local loyalties. The matriarch reflected sadly that the high-ceilinged "living room," whose similarity to the Guggenheim had long ago made it unlivable, had nonetheless been the scene of her children's bar- and bat-mitzvah and wedding receptions; now it was a war room. Family furniture was cleared away, leaving space for more workstations. Bustle bewildered the eye and clamor assailed the ear as legs scurried between desks, hands hammered on computer keyboards, and snarling mouths blared their "Listen up"s, "You gotta be kiddin me"s, and "Fuck outta here"s. The very air reeked of power-lust. Using black and red fonts in its e-memos, the former for issuing orders and the latter for answering subordinates' questions, Ms. Bonnie's new administrative headquarters bore all the trappings of the late republic's bureaucracy, which promulgated the nation's laws and adjudicated the people's disputes—right down to the screens surrounding her desk and the dais upon which it was raised. There was left no doubt as to who ruled from such an Olympus. Minions had to bow or curtsy before entering the inner sanctum. Then they had to look upward to behold her. Ms. Bonnie's computer was mounted on a stand on her desktop, and she worked on her feet. Her natural height was thus added to that of the dais. An electric fan was trained on her forehead. The great hall's snake-themed chandelier hung not far above her head, crowning it, especially when viewed from below, with a blaring Medusan halo, so that Ms. Bonnie's approachers had to shield their eyes, even as they craned their necks.

Tinus Juckman, forgiven for his recent lapse in loyalty, was given a desk too, somewhat to the side. His status could not compare to Ms. Bonnie's. A clearing of the throat was all that was required to approach him. Furthermore, he remained at ground level. He was forbidden to work standing up, though he leapt to his feet whenever Ms. Bonnie summoned him. In spite of his subordination, he was prone to "borrow the tiger's authority." He wore modified tap shoes, for he loved the marching sound they made when he walked. The big hall was a war room, after all, and the effect seemed appropriate. He called his big sister "Governor" and referred to himself as "Judge." (The distinction between executive and judicial prerogatives, apparently, was lost on him; governors and judges were simply powerful people, and that was enough for him.) He called himself "Judge," even when in conversation with real judges. None of the latter objected to the imposture, finding it rather flattering. In fact, he had the full style, "Judge Tinus," embroidered on every suit jacket he owned. The stitching was florescent pink; all his suits were green. He owned thirty-one of them, to cover all the days of the month. On formal occasions, furthermore, he wore a peruke.

So credentialed, "Judge Tinus" went immediately to work: He posted a proscription list, containing the names of those among the family's underlings he deemed to be insufficiently devoted. Insulating herself from this dirty work, Ms. Bonnie gave him full discretion. Those anathematized were subject to interrogation. Judge Tinus presided over these proceedings as well. Unsurprisingly, any potential friend of Micah's fell under the heaviest scrutiny. Each suspect of this description was tailed, and if his path ever diverted to Federal Hill, then his name would be entered on the dreaded register. (Ironically, the list was posted where Micah's bar-mitzvah picture had been displayed.) Several persons so identified would be brought in at once or simply called aside, if they already worked at Velvet Valley Way. The alleged recalcitrants were summarily flogged until dead. Bamboo poles from unassembled shelf units were used to do the work. The beatings took place in the changing room adjoining the swimming pool, which was floored with tile and easy to clean. (In fact, Judge Tinus usually had enough time for an unwinding dip during the mopping.) Hearses replaced ambulances in the traffic on Velvet Valley Way. Several were needed each week. When these somber vehicles began to attract too much attention, Ms. Bonnie called in a few favors, and USPS vans were provided instead. The vans could cart off three or four corpses at a time, and people assumed that someone on the street was doing a lot of online shopping. Dozens were disposed of in this way.

The purge, though gruesome, was lawful. Tinus Juckman's legal team found ways to justify the harsh and copious punishments. His family's involvement in the educational establishment made this job easier. In most cases, those condemned were found guilty of various "education crimes," in connection with work they'd supposedly performed while employed by Lesson Plan. Owing to the stress placed on education as the foundation of American meritocracy, education offences were taken very seriously. Crimes of this type included rigorous grading of student athletes, rigorous grading in general, deviation from syllabi, noncompliance with assessment procedures, and college recommendation fraud. Death warrants for such malfeasance were signed by administrative judges dispatched by ED—the kind who got on so well with "Judge Tinus" when posted to Velvet Valley Way.

Only Rudy Rutowitz, marked for death, was spared the bamboo, at the personal intervention of Goldie Juckman, who had formed an illicit attachment to him. (We seem to be following the pattern set by Mr. Twain in his drawn-out "Ascent of Vesuvius" in *The Innocents Abroad*. High is our hope that the reader can recall the earlier mention of Rudy Rutowitz. Here's a hint: He was the interior decorator.) Evidently, Goldie too had found a substitute for sibling affection. With Micah out of reach, the kindling of her ardor for the other man was natural. She took a shine to Rutowitz when she spotted him spit-shining the silver-plated spittoon version of the Andy Warhol film *Blowjob* that he'd placed in the billiard room, and the two began sneaking off to discuss art. Many of these discussions took place in the master bathroom, where they began collaborating on a *Guernica* mosaic for the shower floor. Word of this connection began to spread. It had been a whole year since The Ambassador's suspicious passing, and people needed something fresh to whisper about. Goldie's former closeness with Micah remained a juicy topic, and so the new variant, with Rudy now standing in for Micah, quickly gained currency. Gossip of this type was inevitable, considering the amount of time Goldie and Rudy were spending together. The little people at Velvet Valley Way remarked that the water bill had gone up again. (In fact, it had.) Soon they were humming "Rubber Duckie" and performing the well-known tongue-in-cheek simulation of fellatio whenever Goldie passed. Goldie herself never noticed the attention, but she and Rudy were now the talk of the house.

When the gossip reached the ears of Ms. Bonnie, her maternal instinct took over. (We will not discuss her managerial instinct, which led her to regard all lascivious snickering as bad for morale.) She was seized by feelings both powerful and complex. Strong emotions are the lot of mothers in general, but when the mother's children are prodigies like Goldie and Micah, the sentiments can assume baroque proportions. On the one hand, she hated that Goldie was the subject of insinuation; on the other, she was oddly jealous on Micah's behalf. Goldie knew how close the two had always been, even though denial had kept her from recognizing—until now—just how close they were. Her children's estrangement from each other by no means diminished the imperative to do something for both of them, and if anything, the confused state of things made her even more desperate. She had to succor the loyal Goldie, yet she also felt the need to protect Micah—even though he was a traitor to Bonnie herself and quite unfaithful to Goldie—from feeling betrayed by his sister.

Declaring that, as an old woman, she could afford to sacrifice her reputation, she resolved to take her daughter's place in the scandal. Martyrdom, therefore, turned out to be a serviceable arrow, though perhaps an arrow of last resort, in Bonnie Juckman's formidable quiver of winning strategies. Why do the things we do, Bonnie asked herself, if not for our children? At any rate, her decision was made.

Judge Tinus called all the Juckman family employees to the main hall for a special announcement. Phones and printers were silenced. The anticipation was palpable as Ms. Bonnie stood upon her dais. While the minions shuffled, their employer cleared her throat and said what she had to say. For the sake of her family's future, Ms. Bonnie swore that Rutowitz had been her paramour and hers alone. It was unnecessary for the daughter to suffer for the sins of the mother. No salacious whisperings concerning Ms. Goldie would henceforth be tolerated. "Leave my daughter alone," Ms. Bonnie said, "for she's as innocent as the day she was born." There was nary a titter among the assembled domestics, as they absorbed her words. Ms. Bonnie's gravitas, and the respect she commanded, carried the day. The empress had laid herself bare, yet none of her court would dare call attention to her nakedness. In the following days, gossip about Goldie ceased.

Although the matriarch thus succeeded in shielding her faithful daughter, her actions encouraged the machinations of her wayward son. Bonnie's gambit had only half succeeded, and as far as Micah was concerned, it had backfired. Micah rubbed his hands. If he was conscious on any level that Bonnie's handling of the Rutowitz business had been intended at least partly to save face for him, he didn't acknowledge it; what he acted upon was his perception that Bonnie was weak. Given a chance to kick Bonnie while she was down, the young Juckman concocted a masterful scheme. Unlike Bonnie's recent maneuver, Micah's stratagem was contrived to benefit no one but himself—or maybe just to injure others, whether he benefited or not. The plot, though convoluted, was easy enough for Micah's intriguing mind to conceive, but its execution required acting ability. Thereupon, he took a drama class at UMBC and proceeded to employ the skills he learned. Feigning filial piety, Micah inveighed against Rutowitz as the seducer of his mother, yet his true purpose was to attack her indirectly by neutralizing the bothersome "Judge Tinus." No one would see where the real blow was intended to fall. An avid re-reader of *Dune*, Micah had hatched a veritable plan within a plan. With so much time on his hands, he had few other outlets for his cleverness. Once again, his strategy was to alienate his rivals from one another. And once again, his purpose was not so much divide and rule as it was divide and hurt. *Let Mom feel lonely too*, Micah said to himself. Apparently, the solace afforded by his Federal Hill jacuzzi was not enough for him.

Micah composed a false affidavit, serpentine in its misdirection, which he submitted to the Baltimore County Circuit Court. He retained no legal counsel, relying entirely on his own perverse talents. Here is where the acting came into play. (Truth be told, he needed barely a moment to "get in character," his natural emotions accustomed as they were to dramatic expression.) He arrived at the county seat of Towson heavily caffeinated. The artificial stimulation not only helped him focus but also enhanced the jerkiness of his movements, making him seem dangerously combustible and all the more demanding of redress. His eyes were red from rubbing. He whipped out the affidavit from his breast pocket and launched into his skit. Prostrating himself on the courthouse floor, he wailed that he had no choice but to air his family's dirty laundry in public, hoping only that justice would be done. He begged forgiveness for his agitated state. He was a desperate man, thinking only of his loved ones. "The fact is that my family has been grievously wronged," Micah shrieked, "not only by a degenerate interior decorator but also by my pimp of an uncle, who has shirked his responsibilities to my poor mother, leaving her exposed and forcing her to pay the price for her own victimhood."

"My poor mother!" was a phrase Micah had never uttered before, yet his performance on this occasion was prodigiously larded with it, and it proved decisive. America still had a heart for its mothers, especially its widowed ones, so Micah's miserere tugged at the right heartstrings. It even convinced Micah himself, and his crocodile tears turned human. The case moved forward. Both Rutowitz and Tinus Juckman were forthwith arrested and tried, and the jury ruled in favor of Micah's testimony. He saw no need to tinker with a winning script. "My poor mother!" worked on this occasion as well. It was a thrilling result, the culmination of months of hard work. Micah's face was busy at the reading of the verdict, as he sobbed while licking his lips. He employed a few sheets of Kleenex, to conceal his mouth as it broke character. "Got 'em," he exulted between sniffles. Beneath his seat, he clicked his heels in triumph. The presiding judge had Rutowitz strangled to death and Tinus Juckman punished for allowing the disgrace of his sister. As had been the case with Arnold Kiester, no appeal was filed. No one questioned the severity of the sentences, in the atmosphere of indignation that Micah had cultivated. Again, young Juckman knew what he was doing. It was a devastating victory for family values. Furthermore, it was victory for patriarchal family values, then enjoying a desperate resurgence in the ongoing Age of Anxiety, as it reaffirmed a brother's responsibility for his sister and thwarted Bonnie's attempt to assume responsibility as a mother. Bonnie and Goldie Juckman kept their grievance and grief to themselves. Bonnie's plans for new business ventures were once again put on hold.

Although Uncle Tinus was then in his sixties, he survived his sentence of one hundred strokes of the bamboo and one hundred days in cangue. (Both ordeals took place at State Circle in Annapolis.) Glad to be alive, he smiled grimly on the day of his release. Friends School now offered him his old coaching job, banking on the publicity; but Tinus was a broken man and could imagine only one venue for his recuperation. Once more, he returned to his place in the Juckman mansion.

Despite his great victory, Micah Juckman found himself obliged to amscray.

By the time Uncle Tinus limped home, popular opinion had evolved in ways that a certain young man, with an eye for the main chance but with no humanist understanding, could not have prognosticated. *I thought America loved a winner*, this young man groused. Despite his clever maneuvering, Micah Juckman was now execrated throughout the community as the one who had brought calamity upon both his uncle and his mother. He'd misread public opinion. Village scorn for Tinus and Bonnie, upon which Micah had placed such grand expectations, proved fickle. *I guess what America really loves is a victim.* His young playmates deserted him. The minority among them who suspected him of poisoning Danielle had excused his conduct on the grounds that he had merely prevented his wife from spoiling his fun; but now he just seemed mean, and the whole cohort of sweet things found it hard to relax in his presence. There were plenty of hot-tubs elsewhere that didn't come with morbid associations like strangling and flogging. When the partying crowd pronounced Micah uncool, his stock began to plummet in general. Tinus Juckman added grease to the fire by tweeting a satirical poem entitled "For Micah." Although Tinus had never tried his hand at poetry before, "For Micah" came to be ranked among the finest verse of the late republic. It was composed with the help of Google Elizabethan. The clever dingus could even pun with the poem's title. "Like cheap glitt'ring plastic, thou know'st no shame," ran one of its lines. "Your smile dost but laminate, your presence contaminate," ran another. Now The Ambassador's son drew the sort of stare he had no wish to draw. Baltimore, where everyone knew everyone, was a poor place to lay low.

Micah was constrained to leave town on his own, and it was over a year before he ventured to return. He took few of his possessions with him, indulging a long-postponed desire to try roughing it, and he climbed into his Lotus Europa with only a backpack. "Oh, well," he exhaled, "Now I get to see the world." Any place where he could be a Micah without being a Juckman would be an improvement. "Got a wife and kids in Baltimore, Jack," he sang to himself, as he drove off. If the irony of the lyric unsettled him, it was only on an unconscious level. As the reader will remember, Micah had murdered both his wife and his kid.

Goldie Juckman longed to make everything right again.

Bonnie Juckman's family had been decimated. It was hard to grasp how things had fallen apart so totally. On the one hand, it was as the Daoists say: Only what is empty can be filled, and only what is scarce can increase, but the brimming cup can only spill its contents, and what is held in abundance can only be lost; on the other hand, it was nothing but a prosaic fact that the family had been ripped apart in a power struggle. Whether viewed philosophically or concretely, the Juckman family's reality was the same. Long divided against itself, it was now scattered to the winds. The dispersal was worse than the discord, per se, because it felt more final.

Of course, as far as Bonnie was concerned, Micah's absence was probably for the best, yet it still imparted a sense of incompleteness. No mother can ever be resigned to a permanent falling-out with any of her children, and the wounded Bonnie grasped at whatever family she had left. Only Goldie remained as close to her as ever. It was Goldie's nature to be supportive, and recent events had enhanced her sense of obligation. Mother and daughter had already done much for each other— with Bonnie, after all, sacrificing her reputation for Goldie's sake— but the psychological toll on Goldie, Bonnie was sorry to observe, was still quite heavy. As torn up as Goldie was, however, she never succumbed to self-pity. Although Goldie was now increasingly prone to behave erratically, her sympathy for others remained her most consistent virtue. It would see her through the current crisis by keeping her attention focused outward, where there was no point in brooding and where the possibilities for making herself useful yet abounded. The main part of her sympathy was reserved for her surviving parent. It was clear that Bonnie, iron woman that she was, had been dealt a series of shocks. The more the mother ground her teeth in frustration, the more the daughter ached in her own heart. Thereupon, the younger woman now spent most of her time at Juckman Manor, handling clerical tasks for the family business, waiting on the proprietress, but above all keeping her company. Goldie always sought to help. During these dark months, she was an invaluable source of succor for Bonnie.

As loyal as she was to her mother, though, Goldie was aware that the happiness of her family depended on the happiness of all of its members. That included any missing ones, whose absence was the chief source of trouble for those yet present, Goldie knew. This awareness turned her thoughts to Micah, the person who claimed perhaps the second-largest share of Goldie's sympathy and who excited additional emotions as well. Private and domestic concerns reinforced each other in the young woman's mind. Goldie still desired nothing more than to bring Micah back into the fold and thereby to effect a permanent reunion, yet she was hard pressed to devise a practical plan. For all her will, she lacked a way. How does one reconcile two loved ones who are at such loggerheads? No answer presented itself, as desperately as she craved one. The weeks wore on, and a long winter of discontent seemed in store. All Goldie could do was to remain attuned to Bonnie's pain. If Bonnie was glum, then Goldie was bound to be even more so.

Help arrived from a crafty quarter.

Goldie's cousin Dylus Schumacher soon volunteered to render whatever assistance he could. Although Goldie had not solicited his aid, he was sensible to the Juckmans' plight and believed himself capable of providing far more than moral support. Sometimes a cousin Dylus is the only one who can break a stalemate. The ability to think outside the box is a distinct advantage, and Dylus was known to make the most of it. Goldie wondered why she hadn't turned to him before. Chiding herself, she realized that she was too accustomed to bearing burdens on her own.

Though not as close to her as Micah was, he was no stranger. They were related on her mother's side and attended the same synagogue on the High Holy Days. Dylus was by nature a very helpful person. (The reader will have noted that "helpful" is as ambiguous as "good," which we discussed in reference to The Ambassador.) "Dylus Schumacher, at your service," was how he introduced himself, which never failed to delight each new acquaintance. He always followed up the self-introduction with a plan for the maximization of advantage. Family, furthermore, meant a lot to him. The various Juckmans, Schumachers, and others with whom he had any dealings, even very occasional dealings, were many in number, yet he made a point of remembering their names and diverse witty things they may have said. (He dispensed with the "at your service" when dealing with family members, but they knew it was implied.) Of course, the closer the degree of family relation, the more helpful he was prepared to be. He had often proved of great service to his father, Hyman, in the furtherance of various chicaneries in the Baltimore-Washington metropolitan area. Most of these capers fit the description of quick real estate flips, sometimes involving the withholding of taxes, the repurchase of the seized property at great discount, and the freezing out of minority partners. From there, his ambition grew. The law, and its exploitation, soon became his niche. He specialized in creating dummy corporations for the purpose of securing FEMA relief, in the aftermath of hurricanes and other disasters. To him it was manna from heaven. His efforts in this field earned him the sobriquet "Storm Tracker." He acquired a fleet of vintage sports cars, chiefly '66 Mustangs, which he garaged free of charge in FEMA equipment shelters.

A Federal grand jury had indicted Dylus for fraud, but before his trial could begin, he skipped bail. (It was, of course, a dummy corporation that had bailed him out.) Coincidentally, Hurricane Dylus was passing through Baltimore at the time, distracting the authorities and thus covering his escape. In fact, he retrieved one of his Mustangs from a generator storage facility, under the noses of its overworked staff. He too sang "Got a wife and kids in Baltimore, Jack," as he absconded. FEMA-issued coupons ensured his access to conventional gasoline, wherever he passed. Together with his namesake hurricane, he tracked north. No law enforcement assets could be spared to mount a search for him.

He made his way to New York, where he contrived to assume the identity of a Columbia student named Ruckleshaus Schumacher (no relation), who had just died. The camouflage was just what the fugitive needed. Dylus had been investigating the possibility of faking his own death, when he came across Ruckleshaus's obituary. (Apparently, the poor schmuck had died of chagrin when he mispronounced the name of Pupin Hall and people laughed at him.) Federal anti-bias rules limited the number of investigations that could be carried out against individuals of the same surname, particularly if the surname in question was regarded as "ethnic;" and because the Schumacher caseload was already maxed out— in fact, it had been maxed out by Dylus—the new Ruckleshaus Schumacher evaded punishment. Authorities had no choice but to substitute Dylus's name for Ruckleshaus's on the death certificate, for the person claiming to be Ruckleshaus—as long as he was a Schumacher—could not be deprived of his civil rights. The late Ruckleshaus had been an MPA candidate, and it was easy enough for the new Ruckleshaus to jump through the remaining hoops of the program and thus to secure the credential. So now "Ruckleshaus Schumacher" was also a "Master of Public Administration." So disguised, he sat for the Unified Civil Service Exam and soon found himself Chief Environmental Compliance Officer of the 101st Airborne Division, concurrently electronic archivist for Christian County, Kentucky. Both jobs were eminently exploitable. (He bought a nice house equally convenient to Fort Campbell and the county archives. Naturally, he obtained reimbursement for both commutes.) In the former capacity, Ruckleshaus discovered that he could bribe the Screaming Eagles' CO to ground all aircraft and thereby reap a fortune in carbon credits. After taking half of the windfall for himself, the remainder was distributed among influential officers according to rank. In the latter capacity, he created a false ancestor, Jeremiah Schumacher, who supposedly was one of the first settlers of the region. On the strength of this fraud, Ruckleshaus received a "Pioneers of Kentucky" vanity plate, among other perquisites.

Home on leave, he played on Goldie's concern for her brother, saying, "You understand Micah pretty intimately, don't you? I've heard he's your bosom buddy." He giggled lasciviously. The aromatherapeutic rose ganache candle, placed equidistantly between them on the kitchen table where they chatted, flickered and sparked. There was a twinkle in his eye. He seemed to be salivating. He didn't need to say "At your service," but Goldie could tell he had a plan. She knew he wouldn't divulge it all at once, though, that he preferred revealing his genius in a dialectic, as though lining up shots in an easy tennis match.

Goldie returned, "Are you *intimating* something, Cousin Dylus? You seem to have something on your mind." The two had been sipping dirty martinis, but now Goldie set her glass down. She looked up at her cousin with her most inviting "complete me" countenance.

The other's expression neutralized and became businesslike. It was time for him to stop the preliminary insinuations and to zero in on the point. He'd already finished his drink and made ready to dispatch the olive. "I'm not just trying to rib you about Micah," he started. "Nothing like that; I'm just wondering if you can sense what he's expecting you to do for him. You should know him at least as well as I do. Someone like Micah loves to mess things up and then wait for others to pick up the pieces." He nodded, for emphasis. "By the way, my name is Ruckleshaus. Dylus is dead." He stripped the olive off the little plastic cutlass with his teeth. Playing about the pimento with his tongue, he managed to say, "So Micah made his little mess, and if Mommy isn't going to clean it up, then that leaves you, Big Sister."

"What can I do for him, after what he did to Mom and Uncle Tinus?" Goldie asked the question in a pleading tone, expecting Ruckleshaus to provide the solution eventually, after she first elaborated on the difficulties. "Don't you remember how he behaved?" She was about to berate Micah for dragging family business before the court, but then she realized that Bonnie had used the court to discipline Tinus, and so she focused her indignation on Micah's histrionic performance under oath. "He was like a monster. I don't know how many times he said 'My poor mother!' all phony like that. It makes me sick just to think of it."

Goldie took a deep breath, no longer for effect but because she was becoming genuinely upset. "Even if I could make a case with Mom for bringing him back, nobody else in the family would go along with it, and I can see why. Micah's bad news, not just because he's scary—I mean, he's like totally gone off the deep end—but also because, I mean, he makes us look bad. Who wants to be associated with him? I mean, do you? He's grade-A poison." Goldie now tried to steady herself and dropped her voice at least an octave. "We Juckmans are supposed to be respectable. Well, Micah flushed all that down the toilet. His reputation would drag us all down." Goldie's lament ended there. She looked off to the side, her gaze unfocused. After a few reflective ticks of the clock, she returned her attention to the faux-wicker aluminum kitchen table (another of Rudy Rutowitz's acquisitions) and reached for her martini. "As much as I miss him, we should probably count our blessings that he's gone." Goldie fluttered her eyelids. She sniffed. Then, after raising her glass to no one, she finished off her martini.

Ruckleshaus smiled. Whether or not Goldie had been calculating when giving vent to her hopelessness, he found it nearly aphrodisiacal and, savoring the moment, made ready to ride to her rescue. He had an eye for human pathos and believed himself above it. This feeling of superiority was a big part of why he was always so happy to help others. *Jesus, these people desperately need me*, he thought to himself. *Doesn't anybody else know? The way out of any situation is to think big.*

"You really are naïve, cousin. The solution is obvious." The way he spoke made everything seem easy. "Just ask yourself what you need and then go get it. It's a simple question of resources. When in doubt, make sure you have enough of them. Resources solve problems. The best resources are powerful people, and if you have enough of them on your side, then a little problem like family reputation will go bye-bye. All we need to do is to find a powerful patron, and then reputation won't matter anymore. Do you follow?" He paused, still smiling helpfully. The refrigerator compressor switched off, as though giving way to his oratory. "Come on, Goldie, can't you see it? Follow the train of thought. If we know we need a powerful patron, then we know where we have to go to get one, don't we? Look at a newspaper. Today, the power is in Washington, and the power in Washington is King Kong. He's the big *shtarker*. Get on his friends list, and everything falls into place. No one will whisper anything about the Juckmans anymore." He nodded slowly, to give his cousin a chance to absorb his wisdom. *Damn, someone oughta write a political thriller about me.* He poured himself another martini. He took a sip and licked his lips.

On the other side of the table, the clouds parted. Goldie began to see a way ahead. The corner of her mouth curved upward in a subtle, saucy smile. She allowed Ruckleshaus to refresh her glass. "This is a pretty good batch," she said. She started nodding too. As her anxiety lifted, she almost laughed. Why hadn't she, the daughter of a Washington fixture after whom a building was named, realized that all roads led to DC?

Long live the King.

True to what her cousin had told her, the current Director of the FBI, a eunuch called King Kong, was then at the height of his influence. The name King Kong would later figure prominently in accounts of America's decline, but during his own time he commanded respect and no one deemed his rise improper. He had, in fact, just been named person of the year by Time Magazine. His autobiography, *More Balls Than Most*, sat immobile atop the *New York Times* bestseller list, where it dominated both the political and inspirational genres. Eunuchs like King Kong had capitalized on the great demand for their employment in both the private and public sectors, where they reduced the risk of costly sexual harassment lawsuits. (The final liquidation of the Catholic Church in a class-action settlement served as the wake-up call.) The trendsetter in this regard had been media scion Pharaoh Weinstein, whose self-castration on live MeToo TV had inspired young Kong (then known by his rapist name of Mahatma Montessori) to choose the gelded path to power. Kong's career, in a few short presidential administrations, led him to his current commanding position in the Bureau.

In Philadelphia's Fairmount Park, King Kong Coliseum was being built in his honor. In spite of Kong's popularity, the prospect of his namesake Coliseum had occasioned an outbreak of the not-in-my-backyard phenomenon. Not a single Philadelphian wanted it there, and so the federal government invoked the doctrine of eminent domain, which by then was used only to build sports venues anyway. Legal formalities concluded, the plans for the Coliseum went forward. The state of the art facility, when completed, would house the Phillies, Eagles, and 76ers, which teams would all be renamed the Philadelphia Eunuchs. (Of course, college athletic teams had been courting Kong's favor in this way for years.) The Coliseum would be wired with 12G technology, permitting sports fans to check their social media accounts, watch videos, trade stocks, and play online games. It was anticipated that a family of four would be able to enjoy pro sports at the Coliseum for a mere five thousand dollars per event—less if they went without mustard for their hot dogs.

Supervising the work was the eunuch Cheops, whose friendship Ruckleshaus Schumacher had cultivated. The intriguing "Rucklemucker" (as Cheops often called him) first noticed the eunuch almost as soon as the latter's testicles had dropped (to the floor), which permitted him to serve as team doctor for USA Gymnastics and thus to begin his rise within the athletic establishment. Ruckleshaus was merely angling for allies among the castrocracy, of course, but in the event, he really liked Cheops. They shared a sophisticated sense of humor. The two would often hold drinking contests to see who could eat a Philly cheesesteak sub with one hand (the game had started as a joke about masturbation), and in the alcoholic atmosphere, Cheops brought Ruckleshaus into the Coliseum project. Though he bore no formal title and counted only as a friendly advisor to Cheops, the point was that Ruckleshaus had come to stand under the grow-light cast by the King himself. It was this political windfall that Ruckleshaus now proposed to share with Goldie. Goldie assented, and Ruckleshaus acted.

Ruckleshaus prevailed upon an MFA student named Wanda Trale to inscribe a commemorative couplet for the Coliseum's main gate, and then he summoned Morgan Schwartzenberg, Goldie's shifty husband, to present the inscription to the stadium authority. Ruckleshaus picked Morgan to play this leading role because 1) he was a nobody and 2) he was uninvolved in recent scandal: The former virtue ensured that he would function as a political pass-through, delivering all the prestige to his in-laws while retaining none for himself; the latter one reduced the chance that negative publicity would rain on the parade. "Just don't fuck this up, Morgan," Ruckleshaus encouraged him, "and you and Goldie and all the Juckmans will have it made." Morgan dutifully attended every scheduled rehearsal for the ritual, and he listened *ad nauseam* (i.e. twice) to Elgar's *Pomp and Circumstance* marches, to condition himself to perform with decorum.

The presentation ceremony took place on a Sunday morning. The pitiless winter sun bleached all upon which it glared, suffusing everything on Earth with a harsh, sickly haze. It was King Kong's birthday, which Congress had declared a national holiday. Of course, the holiday would actually be observed on Monday, but the coincidence of the Director's birthday and the Sabbath for the current year's celebration inspired many churches to schedule special rites; and the Coliseum dedication was in fact attended by many, Morgan included, who had come directly from them. Morgan, accompanied by Goldie, managed to carry himself with all due reverence. His multicultural cross-emblazoned yarmulke, donned during the church service, remained bobby-pinned in place. He climbed out of the limousine, adjusted his kilt, and advanced through the topiary garden to stand before the gate. Advised to leave off his usual Alfred E. Neuman smile, he maintained the gravest, grimmest visage. He pulled a rope, and a pair of red, white, and blue banners fell away, each revealing two lines of Ms. Trale's work on each side of the archway. Ruckleshaus had specified that Wanda's lettering embody a simple stateliness, but he couldn't refrain from "sexing up" the presentation. The Romanesque calligraphy was surrounded by light chasers. (The sparkling effect induced seizures in two of the VIPs.) The inscription read: "Erected to the People's Man / By Every True American / In Thanks for his Sagacity / And Monumental Modesty." It was all so impressive that a wave of enthusiasm swept through the formality-deadened crowd. Morgan beamed, and the assembled gentry applauded. King Kong's pleased countenance smiled down from a billboard-sized plasma screen (for he was proverbially too indispensable to be spared from DC). A brass band began playing, and seventy-six pigeons were released. They circled above the reviewing stand in a churning mass like a tornado. The twenty-one gun salute shot one of them down. It landed in the lap of Pennsylvania state senator Topher "Jackie" Kennedy, who wore his blood-stained pink dress on a special edition of *Entertainment Tonight* that very evening, making him a shoo-in for governor.

Cheops noted these solemnities in a formal letter to Washington, in which the names of Morgan Schwartzenberg and Goldie Juckman figured prominently. Puffing things up a bit, he said that the ceremony would not have been the success that it was, without the couple's punctilious participation. The letter was especially well received at the J. Edgar Hoover Building. (As eunuchs were favored administrators, their correspondence was always read first.) King Kong tweeted his thanks to Cheops for a job well done, and he also praised Morgan and Goldie as just the right kind of community representatives it was so important to have on board. As a special token of appreciation, he included a Photoshopped image of himself standing between them with his arms around their shoulders, inviting them to "use it however they wish." The tweet made homepage (in lieu of front-page) news at the *Baltimore Sun*. More prominent media carried it as well.

In gratitude for his family's honorable mention, Ruckleshaus Schumacher lavished Cheops with pearls, rhinoceros horn, ivory, and several hundred thousand dollars. He also sent the eunuch a fake Rolex certified to have once belonged to Che Guevara. Of course, all of these items (including a cash transaction of that magnitude) were, as the phrase always went, "quite rightfully illegal," but Ruckleshaus was now a made man. Endangered animal products (and national treasures) meant nothing to him. He had no trouble securing the import licenses for the presents, and the cash, he bragged, was "chump change." He was now, as sociologists say, transforming his money into prestige.

As far as Ruckleshaus's relatives were concerned, now that the door was open, it was time to waltz in and get comfortable. A private meeting with their new patron was in order. Goldie Juckman, adorned herself with her best makeup and came to kneel at Cheops' feet. (The Juckmans needed no coaching from Ruckleshaus to realize that it was now Goldie's turn to perform. Since interpersonal skills were now called for, Morgan stayed at home.) Again, it was a Sunday, one week after the calligraphy presentation. The meeting took place in Cheops' office in a tower in the Coliseum, where he sat in a throbbing massage chair. The audience almost opened with a gaffe: The plastic gorilla fists belaboring the back of Cheops' neck made it look like he was nodding his assent at Goldie's approach, and so she advanced toward him prematurely, before he had time to finish his Chef Boyardee hearts of palm capellini primavera as he'd planned; but as soon as he feasted his eyes on Goldie, he forgot his regret at missing the last few bites of his meal and welcomed her eagerly into the room. Goldie thanked the eunuch for allowing the Juckmans to participate in the dedication of his masterpiece. It was an honor her family barely deserved, she declared, and she dropped to one knee as she expressed her hope that she might requite his condescension with a lifetime of devotion. She prayed for his longevity and begged permission to call him "Godfather." "Especially now, with The Ambassador gone," she said, "it's not just me but all my brothers and sisters who need a godfather." Her voice broke most affectingly as she pronounced the title. "We know you are too kind a man to refuse us, no matter how busily you are serving the country." Cheops, as gratified as eunuchs have always been by offers of ersatz fatherhood, kissed her on the forehead. ("Poppa's Got a Brand New Bag" happened to be playing on the stereo as he did so.) In return, Goldie kissed the testicle-sized ruby that adorned the phone case on his belt. They chatted affably over a couple of scoops of Carlo Broschi gelato, and then Cheops walked her up to the drone pad and helped her aboard his favorite ride, a quarter-scale working replica of the *Graf Zeppelin*, which he programmed to take her home.

Everyone in the Juckman family was greatly pleased with its new patron, and Ruckleshaus Schumacher formally lent his name to the alliance by contributing an additional three hundred thousand dollars to have it inscribed—together with his official titles—on the Wall of Donors in the Coliseum. Helping others had always meant helping himself, of course. Now "Ruckleshaus" might as well have meant Superman. As the leading member of Cheops' entourage, he became the drinking buddy, fixer, and procurer for some of the most eminent personages on the East Coast, but he never forgot who his best friend was. He attended the first Philadelphia Eunuchs (baseball) game as Cheops' personal guest and drank champagne out of a batting helmet. Such skybox antics, unfortunately, caused him to miss one of the highlights of the season. He and Cheops were playing the cheesesteak game when Eunuchs slugger Ramon Toballes (an actual eunuch) scorched a line drive into Orioles pitcher Enos Orobicho's groin and ended up with an inside the park home run.

As the Eunuchs dominated the NL East, eunuchs were running the country.

Indeed, Ruckleshaus had attached the family to a rising star, for Cheops' power was irresistible. (Especially with old "Rucklemucker" at his side, his charm was also irresistible.) The scope of his portfolio was widening apace. With a major bit of sycophancy under his belt, how could it have gone otherwise? The eunuch's successful man-

agement of the Coliseum project had catapulted him to chief lieu-
tenant on Director Kong's personal staff, and "the King" (as Kong
was known in Washington) put him in charge of maintaining the
crumbling infrastructure of the East Coast. In his new role, he was
ubiquitous. On a typical day, Cheops could be seen alighting from
his helicopter a good half dozen times in as many states, performing
surprise inspections of his orange-vested workers, who competed for
his attention by "motioning and swearing in all directions until no
one knew his own business."

If Cheops didn't always inspire efficiency in person, he could recognize it in others, even (or particularly) if they weren't human. He
encouraged his labor foreman, a demobilized Postal Service android
called Funk J. Death (for the user ID of the Halo 17 player who'd created his prototype), to assume responsibilities outside his nominal
area of oversight. It was an inspired policy. As Death was nonunion-
ized, he was an ideal candidate for side jobs. Cheops could just tell
him to do something and he would do it as surely as night followed
day. Many of these unscheduled tasks focused on law and order (emphasis on the latter), for how can infrastructure function without
them? "Highways," King Kong liked to say, "used to be called the
King's highways, so no one would fuck with them." Indeed, rebuilding
respect for institutions like interstate highways, Cheops exhorted his
staff, was as important as rebuilding the highways themselves. "Otherwise, you're looking at anarchy." On one occasion, Death spotted
a college student named Cleef Apocka in the act of relieving himself
in public, from a distance of over a hundred paces. (Apocka was fond
of marking his territory; he once peed on Peadon Bridge, near Baker,
Florida.) The android was mulling over Cheops' pep talk about respect when he detected Apocka's indecency. "Hey, urine!" he might

have thought to himself, and when he determined that the subject was standing in a public place, he concluded that there was a 97% chance that he was committing the criminal act of public urination, a federal offence if it occurred near an interstate highway; and Apocka was shooting off an I-495-EXT overpass in Mashpee, Massachusetts. Catching folks with their pants down was Death's programmed specialty. The place on his chest glowed where his USPS patch used to be. He pounced before the pisher could shake it off. After Apocka zipped up, he tried to excuse his conduct as a piece of performance art, but Death wasn't buying it. The foreman placed Apocka under arrest and had him flogged—both shirt and skin were in tatters — until he came up with a few thousand dollars. Apocka's pay-by-phone app came in handy here, as all he had to do was to touch his Samsung to Death's forehead. The money was used to throw an Employee of the Week banquet for Death, who sat beaming at the head of the table, although he couldn't eat. He couldn't pee either, which meant that he never had to excuse himself from the seat of honor; but he listened carefully to the restrooms at the end of the hall, to ensure that no one dibbled on the floor or forgot to flush—also crimes in a federal event pavilion. Death's keen sensory capabilities were typical of the surveillance technology being deployed by King Kong's FBI and other agencies to "run a tight ship" (the phrase was the Director's motto), as conventional governance collapsed in bankruptcy and partisan paralysis. All Death needed to keep going was a charging station, and there was one in every Dunkin Donuts. In fact, androids like Funk J. Death soon took the place of human police officers, because they could simply be reprogrammed whenever accused of civil rights violations, and they never had to sleep while enforcing martial law. Advantaged by their own particular immunities, androids became as ubiquitous as eunuchs.

Under Cheops' jurisdiction, only the charmed ones, Goldie, Morgan, and Ruckleshaus, enjoyed unrestricted comings and goings; in fact, they were frequent guests at the eunuch's feasts. Whereas ribaldry was the watchword, whenever Cheops was hanging out with Rucklemucker *en paire*, with Goldie and Morgan present, pure gluttony was the object. Unlike Death, Cheops could eat a great deal, and his suppers were sumptuous and social. The repasts, furthermore, were of frequent occurrence. Most of these were crab feasts, as Ruckleshaus could always get ahold of bushels of endangered blue crab. He typically steamed the spiders himself—with a little apple cider vinegar, his secret ingredient—and then summoned the other three to wherever he happened to be. The Cheops-Schumacher-Juckman-Schwartzenberg coterie liked to eat on piers on the Chesapeake Bay, from which, after dispatching each crustacean with relish, they would toss its Old Bay-encrusted shell pieces into the old Bay. It all had kind of a Roman feel about it. Neighbors could only marvel, whispering that the archway at King Kong Coliseum was the means by which the younger generation of Juckmans had aligned themselves with Cheops and thus with King Kong. They were as "made" as could be. "Think where man's glory most begins and ends, and say their glory was they had such friends." They were all having a good time, too, enjoying equal measures of pleasure and protection. Without such patronage, mere mortals lived in fear of a visit from Death or something like him and had to make do with imitation crabmeat. Neither Death nor pulverized whitefish was a concern for the favored ones. Ruckleshaus had been quite right about the indispensability of friends in high places. As a King Kong affiliate, one could skip along without a care.

What few people realized, though, was that the original purpose of such a connection was to effect the rehabilitation of the disgraced Micah Juckman. The family was indeed riding high, but it was still fractured, and no amount of crab feasts with Cheops could make good the sense of incompleteness. Goldie's beloved brother had been laying low for months.

Finally, though, it was becoming possible to imagine that the reunion might take place. Ruckleshaus Schumacher's thinking had been that society's fear of the family's powerful friends would discourage attacks on Micah, were he to resurface, and it was in fact this consideration that induced Micah to come home. The advent of a favorable wind was heralded by the uppermost weathercock. It was King Kong himself who signaled that the coast was clear by expressing regret, in a comment attached to a photo of the latest crab massacre on Ruckleshaus's Facebook page, that the whole Juckman family couldn't be present. The king having spoken, all doubt was removed. Soon all Goldie's hopes were realized as Micah was able to return to Baltimore without so much as a raised eyebrow at his reappearance. That Ruckleshaus was truly a wizard, so clearly did he foresee that the king's grace would wash Micah's sins away. Indeed, to avoid giving the impression that Micah was in any way obliged to sneak into town, Ruckleshaus took it upon himself to stage a splendid soiree at Velvet Valley Way. People who had shunned Micah were now afraid to be absent. Even Bonnie managed a "Welcome back." She sat on a divan flanked by bamboo palms, mimosa in hand and bliss on her lips, surveying the joyous get-together. After the party, Goldie lovingly cleansed Micah of the dust of the world. It could not have been a happier homecoming for all concerned, and, human nature being what it is, feelings of domestic felicity soon turned to anticipation of brighter business prospects, under the restitched Juckman banner. With the Juckman family reunited, it seemed poised for a revival of its fortunes. Bonnie, no longer distracted by her renegade eldest son, was now free to pursue all the opportunities her still-keen vision yet beheld. The house, no longer divided, was now ready to ascend, and all its lamps were lit. All slept soundly that night on fresh linen, with both happiness and riches in their dreams.

The optimism, however, was short-lived. House Juckman was only outwardly reunited. The fissures in the foundation proved not so easily mendable.

Can we really expect Micah and Goldie, together or apart, to live happily ever after?

Micah, alas, quickly caused a new rupture, this time with his sister Missy, the late Ambassador Schloss's third daughter. No, Micah didn't force himself on Missy, but his twisted libido was to blame, and it went to work almost immediately. It was Micah's nature, perchance, to waste everything but time. Indeed, nature, not only the aggregate of our tendencies but also the totality of our surroundings—the sun, the rain, the warm air, the green trees—rules over us all. It happened in the springtime, when globular morning-stars of DNA form sickly yellow clouds in the air, blurring the line between fertilization and infection. A certain anticipation hangs heavy in the spring sky as well, thwarting all hope of contentment. Some will always be allergic to peace. Love, too, to which Micah had just been restored, often proves, likewise, a pathogen.

Missy Juckman was newly married to the e-journalist Ben Varrick and had hired his young cousin Riggi as her personal assistant. It was hard to say whether husband or aide brightened Missy's life the more. Riggi proved to be a godsend, particularly in the realm of decluttering, on one occasion persuading Missy that she didn't need specialized whole-, skim-, soy-, almond-, and macadamia nut milk frothers. Riggi also classified Missy's food photos (Missy couldn't eat without preserving each appetizer, entrée, or dessert in a jpeg), cross-referencing them by date, state, and Michelin rating. Missy was both satisfied and impressed with the capable Riggi and found herself making plans for the girl's future. Such an inclination was very Schlossian. The idea that a bright young person would naturally go places while still needing help over natural obstacles was worthy of the old Ambassador and his paradoxical twentieth-century conception of merit. In addition to career advice (which proved superfluous, Riggi possessing a strong sense of direction), Missy also tendered assistance in the romantic department. A consummate matchmaker, Missy introduced Riggi to her meditation coach, Razia, and the two were soon engaged. Missy was quite pleased with herself, for the match was indeed a happy one (and was also, as shall be seen, a durable one). Riggi and Razia had a lot in common, despite the former driving an e-tron and the latter an I-Pace, and so they decided to tie the knot after a couples therapist convinced them both to buy i3s. They installed a dual hers and hers charging station in their driveway, in case they both needed juice at the same time. The wedding was planned for late summer, and then the couple hoped to go to grad school together. Not even their disparate specialties could wrench them apart. Riggi was interested in Mossynoecian Studies and Razia wanted credentials to teach vegan tin drum composition to the Naxalite diaspora of the Loire valley; fortunately, both found suitable doctoral programs at MIT. They were well-embarked on their journey to the good life.

Micah Juckman, however, made his characteristic advances upon Riggi and promptly got her pregnant. It was immaculately done. Although Micah wore three condoms, conception occurred accidentally when he vomited his own semen into Riggi's vagina. The fateful spew also included a school of half-digested King Oscar sardines, but Micah was able to suck those back out. Riggi was a reliable lesbian, but she enjoyed exploring her power over men; in this case, the exploration bore unexpected fruit. In fact, it was a strong reaction against the smell of fruit—jackfruit, pretty pungent stuff anyway—that gave Riggi the first inkling that she was pregnant. Riggi decided against an abortion, because she had recently adopted a Pomeranian named Fetus and couldn't bear the thought of aborting anything called fetus. She resolved to have the baby.

Though Micah was desirous of making Riggi his mistress, Missy would not indulge him and determined to keep her out of Micah's clutches. Micah protested—not out of any love for Riggi or for his unborn child but only in the heat of the argument—but Missy was unmoved. Missy relocated Riggi to a secret apartment and kept her on salary. She never visited Riggi, for fear that Micah would follow her to the safe house. Of course, the affair was none of Missy's business—Razia forgave Riggi and looked forward to raising the child with her; and Riggi could take care of herself, as far as Micah was concerned—but the sibling rivalry was so strong that Missy was revolted at the idea of Micah having his way. Too much had been sacrificed already on the altar of Micah's feelings. *Not this time, Hermano*, she thought to herself. Dwelling on the issue, she soon worked herself into a rage and began abusing Micah on social media, calling him King Oscar, among other epithets. Thus was opened a war of words between brother and sister. As it increased in bitterness, the other Juckmans could only duck for cover, clinging to the just-recovered peace by giving Missy and Micah a wide berth. An unfortunate climax was reached when they bumped into each other at Velvet Valley Way (where Missy still lived and from whence Micah was again moving out). Micah renewed his entreaties concerning Riggi, and the entreaties soon turned into demands and then threats. "No, Micah, you can't just fuck my secretary and then live with her happily ever after," she barked at him. It was really the first time he'd been denied in such point-blank terms (after all, he'd always been able to fuck and live with whomever he wanted), and he took it quite badly. Micah reached into the box he was carrying and threw the first thing he grabbed, a pornographic mahjong set he'd acquired during his travels, at Missy's head. It missed her and burst open against the wall, sending colorful shrapnel—phallic bamboos, vulvic flowers, and amorous birds of prey—ricocheting off the walls of the hallway and clattering cacophonously to the floor.

Because Ben Varrick, as the expression still went, came from money, Ruckleshaus Schumacher, with his keen concern for the Juckman family's interests, was anxious to avoid a larger falling-out. The Juckmans themselves were both overinvolved and exhausted, giving Ruckleshaus yet another chance to make himself useful. *This new scandal*, Ruckleshaus calculated, *could cost us mucho resources, and if Varrick writes anything about us, it's all over.* "Let's all just take it easy. No one wants to have to take sides here," he addressed the young Juckmans and their spouses Ben and Morgan in a tense conference in the "living room." "Remember The Ambassador's legacy. There's still a lot we can do as a family, if we just sweep all this under the rug. That means the two of you have to cool it," he said with helpful nods to Missy and Micah. He intervened in the siblings' quarrel and was finally able to convince Micah that his covetousness was unreasonable—and also unwise, given his poor reputation. Ruckleshaus was, as usual, persuasive. The faithful cousin paid a follow-up visit to the rebellious son at the latter's reclaimed digs on Federal Hill. They were the only two in the hot tub, and the sober atmosphere permitted rational discussion. "Let's not forget how much we're hoping for people to forget," Ruckleshaus advised Micah. "We should take the long view. We've got to stay out of the spotlight for a while. As long as things don't blow up again, we can be hottubbing till we're old and gray," In this way was an uneasy harmony maintained. Ruckleshaus then met with Ben Varrick, at a pleasant alfresco luncheon (guarded by Funk J. Death and a few Pinkerton drones) in the grassy space where Harborplace used to be, and got him on board too. As long as Micah behaved himself, Ben would hold his peace. *You're welcome, Cousin Ruckleshaus*, muttered Cousin Ruckleshaus to himself.

Micah stayed away from Riggi and contented himself with boasting about having slept with a girl who didn't shave her legs. Summer came. Riggi and Razia celebrated their wedding as planned. Then, they were off to MIT.

Next, it was Goldie Juckman's turn to be indiscreet. The reader will have remembered the Rudy Rutowitz affair and, furthermore, needs no reminder about geese and ganders; but the point is simply that Goldie was human. She had never been happy with Morgan, and "R²," as Riggi and Razia's wedding was called, made her feel that she was missing out on the love she deserved. Indeed, she was. Having Micah around had not restored things to the way they were, especially given his continued dissolution, and she felt lonelier and more incomplete than ever. Perhaps the old anticipatory shame was to blame for the distance between them. (The siblings' reunion shower was not repeated.)

In any case, the shoe was now on Goldie's foot. She grew fond of the graphic novelist Da'Kara Nahni, a strapping young man who proved of great service to her in the bedchamber, owing not only to his tremendous physical endowment but perhaps even more to his general ingenuity and eagerness to please. They met at a clothing-optional reception for the Tony Award-winning musical *Anne Frank at Bergen-Belsen* and consummated their relationship right there in the Kennedy Center vaping lounge. Da'Kara encouraged Goldie to indulge her creative side. In practice, the creative juices flowed both ways. Many of the coital positions featured in his bestselling *Drill Sergeant* series became numbers in their private repertoire, and vice-versa. Da'Kara, ever the professional, listed Goldie as a consultant for *Drill Sergeant 17: To the Rear, March!* They even got into the cosplay. Goldie typically wore the uniform of the Fifth New York Volunteer Infantry (Duryée's Zouaves), Da'Kara that of the 11^0 Reggimento Bersaglieri, circa 1918—tear-away versions in both cases, of course.

Even while enjoying Da'Kara's company, however, Goldie also had eyes for Ruckleshaus Schumacher's youngest brother, Cyrus, a fiercely handsome man with gleaming, fair skin and a heroic, jet-black beard. The facial hair fascinated her. *Cosplay is one thing*, Goldie pondered, *but I'll bet that beard is real enough not to go crooked when rubbed on the rug.* Their courtship was modern. Goldie noticed Cyrus among Ruckleshaus's Facebook friends, and they began commenting on each other's memes. A masterfully subtle game of escalation ensued. When he posted a grinning squirrel saying TGIF, she liked it; when she displayed a mushroom cloud with a "Who Farted?" he loved it; and when he put up the old photo of Albert Einstein sticking his tongue out, with the caption "It Doesn't Take a Genius to Know How to Eat Pussy," she commented, "ROTFLMA&TO." Goldie struggled to keep her true feelings for Cyrus in check, as the seduction moved from the comment field to the direct message. Lusting for him privately, she intimated that if he became her personal secretary, she would call him big brother. The innuendo thus became specific, no longer about farts or cunnilingus in general but focused squarely on their relationship. Young Schumacher was intrigued. "Personal secretary" appealed to his submissiveness, "big brother" to his urge to dominate. Cyrus lived on the Eastern Shore, but he decided he could learn to like the commute. He had nothing else on his plate, professionally or romantically. Accordingly, he showed up one day with a "Got any envelopes for me to lick?" Not at all taken aback, Goldie assured him that she had a lot of things for him to lick and a list of other needs besides. They began working together in unseemly closeness, by day and by night. While her relationship with Da'Kara was pure raunch, Goldie hoped to cultivate with Cyrus a broader intimacy, not only sexual but sensual, emotional, spiritual; and Cyrus was similarly interested in sharing the whole person. Each liked the way the other smelled. Each liked the way the other smiled. She invited him to sleep at Velvet Valley Way, on the grounds that it would create more time for work. At the time, their relationship was yet unconsummated, for they were prolonging the flirtation phase as long as it could be savored. He said he would bring his toothbrush. Cyrus was aware that Goldie had something going on with Da'Kara—and with his X-rated graphic novels—but the thought of her sexual prowess increased her appeal for him; it was part of the whole person that Cyrus was so eager to share, and the prospect thrilled him.

Goldie's husband, Morgan, naturally suspicious, hacked Cyrus's Facebook account, forged a private message, and tricked Goldie into revealing her adulterous intentions. Born on Facebook, the Goldie-Cyrus liaison had apparently died on Facebook, thanks to a snooping husband. It might have been the cleverest thing Morgan had ever done. (Even so, he had technical help—see below.) The fatal communication was a gif of a scene from *Drill Sergeant*, with Goldie's caption reading "I want you to drill me every day." She'd glitzed it up with the exploding valentine effect. Even though Cyrus's initial PM wasn't really his, he was conscientious enough to reply 👍 to Goldie's invitation.

Goldie's harlotry (at least her premeditated harlotry) was soon splashed all over Facebook, Instagram, and Harlotry. The whole family was scandalized. This is the Juckman family we're talking about, which should have been used to the smell of its own farts by now; but why, all wondered, had Marigold been so careless? To think that Goldie trolled around like that! Not only drills but power tools in general became taboo at Juckman Manor. (Of course, they hadn't been that scandalized when Micah turned his house into a miniature Babylon, but nobody pointed out the inconsistency. Micah himself certainly did not. And yes, there had been that thing with Rudy Rudowitz, but that earlier misstep had at least occurred in person, and decent people—assuming they saw through Bonnie's false confession to the affair—could pretend that Goldie had been seduced. Now they had ocular proof, in horrid Facebookese, of her depravity.)

Morgan Schwartzenberg's social media consultant, Maxwell Norman Aire-Girotua, waxed indignant on behalf of his patron. The situation seemed to him to call for it. His was the perfect, fatal, American combination of prurience and prudery. It set him pacing the floor in Morgan's office. "Bitch," he called Goldie, when it became clear that Morgan wouldn't mind. On the contrary, the curse, applied to his wife, was music to Morgan's ears. "Bitch" is indeed the "Amen" in the ritual of male bonding. Morgan and Aire-Girotua bonded a great deal during those weeks. It was Aire-Girotua who had helped Morgan to hack Goldie's Facebook account. "Facebook is where we'll get 'em, boss," he promised, "because people are still crazy enough to let their guard down there." It was Aire-Girotua who had baited the hook with the forged flirtation—a meme showing an athletic English butler waiting leeringly upon a pixieish countess with the caption "What's your pleasure?" They'd shared a laugh over that one. It was Aire-Girotua also who had leaked the scandal. He catered to Morgan's worst impulses and sometimes even led him on. Now, it was Aire-Girotua who awaited his master's orders. He did so with such palpable readiness that Morgan would have hated to disappoint him.

Morgan said, "Seeing how it's all true, then, I guess I'll have to kill her. Right? There's only so much a man can take. Look at her, running around like that." It seemed the right thing to say. He peered out the window at the sun flaring through the trees. Overwrought aggrievement smothered all his other feelings. His eye twitched. Aire-Girotua begged leave to help with the murder, and Morgan accepted his offer. The social media consultant started snapping his fingers and clapping his palm to his fist, like Curly of the Three Stooges (except that there were only two stooges in the room). Cooling off was now impossible in the ensuing one-upmanship. It was a true pissing match. The two cologne-reeking primates egged each other on, in a crescendoing symphony of machismo. Pizza was ordered. Alcohol, naturally, played its part. Soon, the operational plan emerged. They swore to the plot, with oaths signed in blood. Morgan licked his bloody finger, and his tongue and lips showed red for the moment, making him look like a sated vampire (the flying mammal, not the undead Transylvanian). "Just like in that movie," Morgan rattled, but he couldn't say which one. What other rituals were customary, on such occasions? Morgan wondered if they should post the proceedings on Facebook, but the aggrieved husband's loyal and sensible social media consultant—"Max-Norm," Morgan dubbed him—talked him out of it. "You've done enough brainstorming for one day, boss; now it's time to flesh the thing out. Leave everything to me," he said. He was so thrilled to play the part of the attentive henchman that he shuddered a bit.

Soon, Aire-Girotua had recruited six confederates, and they all gathered at Spike and Charlie's Restaurant downtown to swear further oaths, over a meal of sliced almonds and assorted garnishes. The almond du jour was the Portuguese Pretty Saint Bras, which was served in a single-seed fillet. Customers could choose their own glaze, and Morgan went for one made with Macquarie Island honey. The "Mac," as the house pairing consultant termed it, bonded exquisitely with the meat of the PSB, when the shell was removed. It was the best four hundred and ninety-nine dollar sliced almond that Morgan had ever eaten, which he regarded as a favorable omen. He nodded appreciatively at Max-Norm, seated at his right hand. He picked up the eighteen-inch platter and licked the dribbled glaze off until it was gleaming white.

To all appearances, the cuckold was primed for murder. In his heart, however, Morgan was wavering, not simply because he was afraid of the still formidable Bonnie Juckman, but also because he couldn't, after all, bear the thought of losing Goldie and really had no wish to kill her. His feelings were complex. He loved her once, and he loved her political connections still. What would he, or could he, do without her? This whole revenge thing was getting out of control. The mafia-like comradery and ceremony were fun, but the thought of it leading to violence was unreal. *Can't we just enjoy our almonds and go home? I guess I am a creep, but I don't think I'm a murderer.* He kept his reservations to himself, though, and the band of bravos, having completed their ritual, took their places in the Juckman family compound, outside the cottage Goldie used for her office. The effects of the Syrah they'd swilled at Spike and Charlie's were wearing off. It was a chilly night, and the rumbling trucks on the nearby Beltway filled the air with their lonely moan. The sound filled Morgan with a dismal homesickness. "Velvet Valley Way is going to see a few more ambulances tonight," Aire-Girotua snarled, to boost morale. (Morgan's remained unboosted.) "Heads up, and follow my lead." He performed another Curly Howard castanet gesture.

Soon enough, Cyrus Schumacher appeared and, accompanied by an exotic dancer carrying a tajine of Moroccan chicken and couscous, entered the cottage. (The scandal had forced Cyrus to abandon the plan of moving in, but he and Goldie continued to sneak around.) The dancer was wearing bells, and the jangling of her movements, audible to the goons outside, provided a final few notes of incitement. *Well, they really are a couple of perverts.* The ambuscaded men passed a final "tsk-tsk" among themselves and emerged from cover. They stomped, rather than tiptoed, through the tulips that Goldie and

Cyrus had had planted alongside the walkway to the cottage. Morgan stepped forward too but hesitated, disbelieving what was happening. His hands started shaking, his legs stopped carrying him forward, settling into a pacing pattern, and he never crossed the threshold.

Max-Norm Aire-Girotua and the six bravos then burst into the house, stripped all three of its occupants, and began beating them. The victims were too surprised to put up any kind of a fight. One of the invaders turned up the stereo, to make the fracas sound like a party. 98 Rock was playing the ELO classic, "Evil Woman": *You made a fool of me; but them broken dreams have got to end.*

Aire-Girotua had picked his men well: computer geeks of the help desk who resented having to deal with demanding, pampered nincompoops like Goldie Juckman every time they wanted to do a mail merge. Forsooth, their sense of grievance was well-developed. Velvet Valley Way, furthermore, presented a pageant of privilege and indulgence that common folk dreamed of despoiling. Added to this general class hatred was a personal grudge, because a few of them had been in the house before, to set up a 4D *Drill Sergeant* screensaver for Goldie's monitor, and her behavior on that occasion, while not at all rude, had been plenty condescending. It was because of Goldie's reputation for haughtiness, and because the dancer was so young, that their attackers were determined to strip them naked. Thus did the tornado sweep through the main room, casting torn clothes through the air. The dancer's bells issued a final clang as the men threw her costume to the floor. They picked it up again and shredded it for good measure. They stripped Cyrus Schumacher too for complex reasons of self-hatred and jealousy, but once he was un-clothed, they kept their distance and focused their violent attentions on the females. Animal instinct took over, though not so completely as to challenge the definition of man as a social animal. As savagely as they behaved, the attackers' social urge to humiliate remained the chief driver of their lust, and they slugged and kicked so as to make their precious victims as ugly as everyone else. Their abandoned state by no means precluded lawyerly calculation. After the women were dead, so the men's reasoning went, their corpses could be speedily redressed, to avoid the appearance of impropriety. Plugged into several media feeds 24-7, they had internalized society's revulsion at sex crimes. The jackals were nothing if not pious. Believing themselves righteous avengers, they didn't want people to think that *they* were the perverts. Not that anyone really cared how things looked. The only look that mattered was that Princess Goldie and her friends ended up looking undesirable. *Let people think we raped them, as long as no one thinks we envied them.* Of course, envy had been their master from the beginning.

One at a time each assailant stepped forward, cudgel in hand. The choruses of "Evil Woman," with their insipid refrain "Evil woman," bracketed by insipid fill-ins, accompanied each help-desk goon as he approached. Flourishing his weapon, each bared his teeth. Then his weapon descended. As the men landed their blows, their bodies throbbed with the brutality of the powerless. "Bitch!" would have been a natural war-cry, but the attackers were too enraged to speak. A few of them began weeping with their exertions, as they discharged lifetimes of frustration and fury. Needless to say, they pulled no punches. Aire-Girotua was especially merciless, dragging his victims across the floor before bludgeoning them. A genius at dealing pain, he made sure to hit their heads on pieces of furniture as he dragged them. He was sweating with the effort. The salty secretion got in his eyes and blurred his vision, but he never lost sight of the chief target. He thrashed the dancer because she was there; but he laid into Goldie Juckman, his master's bitch, like the guard dog he was. For him, it was neither business nor personal; he was trying to prove a point, to put Goldie—and all uppity women—in her place, and it is this motivation that moves its subject to the greatest violence. For all the damage he inflicted with the club, though, he dared not strike her with his hands. Touching her, somehow, would have been too much of a trespass.

Despite the beating, Goldie regained her feet, but even so, her strength began to falter. Each attack now numbed more than it hurt. The room was going dark. All she heard was static. She had taken pilates and yoga but never a martial art. Deep down, though, she possessed vast resources of endurance and resolve. It was only her stubborn willpower that kept her on her feet, even after Aire-Girotua had dragged her before the fireplace. The longer she remained standing, however, the more savagely Aire-Girotua and the others beat her. Though she tried to meet the attacks with her fists, she soon sank again to the ground. Now she was being kicked as well as clubbed. Even prone, though, she remained defiant. Goldie's resilience rested on a firmer sense of injustice than the false aggrievement that so inflamed her foes. *It's not fair*, she thought. *Can't everyone see it? How come Micah gets to have all the fun and nothing happens to him? We worked so hard to get him back, but he just couldn't stop chasing around after . . . others . . .* As the blows rained down, she roared with an animal fury and kicked her feet at her enemies. *Let them see I've got plenty of fight in me; I won't go quietly!* She considered spitting at them but then remembered the proud truism that creeps like Aire-Girotua weren't worth it. Instead, she threw everything—beer bottles, books, potted succulents—she could get her hands on. *At least I'm dying like a man.*

At least I'm going down fighting like a man. All I wanted to do was to fuck like one. In spite of her valiant defense, however, the goons' assault continued unabated, and Goldie continued to fade under the pounding. Finally, she was about to breathe her last. Her dimming eyesight could only make out a few shapes. She looked over at the naked Cyrus and decided it had all been worth it. *He was really going to take me there, when these bozos showed up. Bastards. What rotten timing. Interrupting me like this, just before I try a Moroccan threesie. Well, I guess this is how I would want to go.*

Bonnie Juckman, however, heard the racket and rushed to the scene in her dressing gown. She flew over the walkway as though on a cushion of anger, though her flight was steady. She said nothing. Her face was impassive. She was unattended. Motion-activated lights cast circling quartets of shadows as she crossed the distance from the main house to Goldie's cottage. A faint whiff of Giorgio Armani Acqua di Gioia was the only herald of her arrival. It was enough to alert the busy brutes to her presence. While Morgan, who had been pacing outside the doorway, fell tearfully to his knees at her approach, the ruffians prepared to give the mother the same treatment that they'd been doling out to the daughter. Individually, they wondered whether they would strip Bonnie too; no one wanted to take the initiative, but they would have done it had one of them suggested it. Laying low the mighty, after all, was what they were about. It would be like extra credit. They trooped out of the wrecked cottage one by one, smacking their cudgels against the palms of their hands. The reports echoed throughout the various outbuildings of the suburban estate, the painted brickwork of which bore no muffling ivy. Exhilarated despite their fatigue, they counted on a second wind, as the matriarch came within reach and what Locke called "the spirit of persecution" rekindled in their hearts. Bonnie's perfume continued its provocation, and it looked like more Juckman flesh was about to be bruised.

Ms. Bonnie, however, maintained such a regal bearing that the toughs could not raise a finger to her. Each became as hamstrung as the assassin who had King Gustavus Adolphus in his sights but could not bring himself to pull the trigger ("for as he looked," writes Wedgwood, "his heart would turn to lead and his hand refuse to act"). They hesitated, working their jaws in unreleased anticipation. They looked left and right and at the ground. Each waited for a signal from another, as Ms. Bonnie brushed past him. None even uttered a sarcasm. The old woman's expression could have cut glass. If she recognized Aire-Girotua, she didn't say so. She marched into the house, found Goldie, and helped her back to the main residence. 98-Rock was now playing a pimple cream commercial, which was subdued enough in volume to let the sound of crickets chorus through and accompany Bonnie as she supported Goldie up the stairs. The door closed and the yard lights switched off. The bullies, Morgan included, shuffled around a bit more but soon left without a word.

Ambulances indeed made their way up Velvet Valley Way that night, but none of their passengers died. Bonnie made sure not just Goldie but all three of the victims received the best medical attention. Soon they recovered, though Goldie was the last to be discharged from the hospital.

Bonnie never involved the police, reasoning that the ensuing bad press would hurt her family even more and believing also that she could handle Morgan; however, in the latter assumption she was (at least initially) mistaken, for her son in law, since he'd chickened out during the attack, felt all the more compelled to act manly.

Having failed to murder his wife, Morgan Schwartzenberg took his grievances against her to Maryland governor Socrates Kennedy. Politicians would answer where thugs had failed. He journeyed to Annapolis via rented limousine. (Passing through Severna Park, home of the late Arnold Kiester, should have disillusioned him about "making the system work for me," but he was too blinkered by indignation to make the connection.) The cuckolded husband needed to do *something* to salve his wounded pride. He ordered Alexa to play "Try Again," by Aaliyah, and as he tried again to eat a bacon bagel and follow along with the lyrics at the same time — "If at first you don't succeed, then dust yourself off and try again"—he waxed therapeutically about how sometimes even the best of us have to fall back on Plan B to get what we want. Petitioning the government for redress would have to suffice. "As long as Goldie knows who's boss." Governor Kennedy was a FOKK (Friend of King Kong), and Morgan was hoping that his service to the eunuch faction at the Coliseum would count in his favor. (*That was the whole point, right? What else did I rent the fuckin' kilt for?* argued Morgan to himself. *Now it's time for the FOKKers to do something for me.*)

The hope was a thin one. To be sure, it sprang as eternally as righteous indignation in the wronged one's breast, but it sprang falsely. Morgan, alas, was prone to overrate his own importance. Proximity to eminence had befuddled him, had made him forget that he remained, essentially, a schmendrick. Of course, it was Goldie Juckman and not Morgan who called Cheops "Godfather." It was Goldie who had paid court to him in his skybox. It was Goldie who had kissed the eunuch's ruby-testicled phone case. Goldie's husband could claim no such closeness. Morgan was only Cheops' God-son-in-law, if there even was such a thing. He'd never hung out with

Cheops alone. Morgan wouldn't even have triggered an autofill if Cheops typed "mo" into the address field of any of his text messaging apps.

Morgan also put too much faith in the larger family relationship. Governor Kennedy had indeed held jobs in the Department of Education and had often worked with Ronnie Schloss, but again, the connection would not benefit Morgan directly. (It was not that the Kennedy-Juckman nexus wasn't notorious. The Governor and The Ambassador were as thick, some said, as thieves. Their cooperation had tested the limits of public and private. Together, Socrates Kennedy and Ronnie Schloss had made Lesson Plan the official online learning platform of the state of Maryland. Socrates helped himself to a finder's fee. Good Ronnie never saw the arrangement as corrupt. To him, the winners were Maryland's students.) Strictly speaking, Governor Kennedy could only count as a friend of the Juckman family, of which Morgan Schwartzenberg was at best a peripheral part. He just didn't count as a full-fledged Juckman. Morgan badly overplayed his hand. Maybe we all lose sight of our insignificance, but Morgan, in the heat of the moment, was leveraging weak credentials in a major power play. Had he been thinking clearly, Morgan might have expected to be thrown out of the Governor's office as soon as he announced his name. He almost was. It was indeed difficult for Morgan to get past the Governor's gauntlet of gatekeepers. Pure chutzpah was the only thing that got him through the door— and then, once the Governor set eyes on him, pity did the rest.

In the event, Governor Kennedy adopted a solution meant to save face and minimize damage. He realized that the unstable Morgan presented, at bottom, a management problem. As a reasonable man—and a calculating FOKK—the Governor knew enough to stay focused on the big picture and not to let a little thing like attempted murder cloud his view of it. In fact, the chief object was to prevent the larger public from having any view of it at all. The longer the business dragged on, he considered, the sorrier it would be for everybody. Therefore, let the management begin. *The first step is to give the squeaky wheel his grease. Otherwise, he'll go on squeaking all over town.* Addressing Morgan, the Governor said, "Goldie is Cheops' goddaughter, yes? Cheops, in turn, works for the King. That makes Goldie the protected one, and it's *our* job to protect *her.* Protection is what women want, right?" He cleared his throat. "You're her husband; you should have been protecting her from the beginning." *Let the little rat squirm; he needs it.* "Instead, you let her become the victim," Socrates declared, pausing for a moment to let the rebuke sink in. "Well, then, the proper thing to do is to avenge her shame. The last time something like this happened, Ms. Bonnie stepped up to take Goldie's shame upon herself, but our game isn't martyrdom; it's revenge. That's the *man's* part, *n'est-ce-pas?* You had the right idea, Morton, but you—I mean Morgan—but you went about it all wrong; you weren't subtle. Let's do it discreetly and sweep this whole mess under the rug." Both the Governor and Morgan as well absently looked at the classic Agra rug that covered the floor in the center of the office, as the lecture continued. "If it doesn't stay under the rug, at least we'll be standing on the moral high ground, which is where you want to be, in this business.

"I guess I'm preaching to the choir, because the whole reason you came to me is that you expect me to take care of it better than those help desk creeps; well, all right, then. It should be easy enough to get the death penalty for Cyrus Schumacher. He certainly deserves it. *Sic semper seductores.* But there I go, thinking like a lawyer. In fact, we won't need to go through the courts. We'll just use the eunuch option. The eunuchs are calling the shots these days, and eunuchs can't abide satyrs like Cyrus who can't keep it in their pocket." The solution was almost too obvious.

Governor Kennedy borrowed Funk J. Death to carry out the sentence. It so happened that Death had an open block on his schedule, owing to a cancellation (the coincidentally named Chase Morgan Bank had reached a settlement with the profit watchdog SMAUG— the Society for Making America Unlearn Greed—and so no longer required a visit from the android to shake it down). Recently refurbished as a pilotless drone, Death arrived in Mobtown after flying south above I-95, suspended from his propeller beanie like the Japanese anime character Doraemon the cat. All who saw him shuddered as he passed overhead. Although Death was Cheops' employee, the eunuch had no scruple against lending him out to any fellow FOKK. He never expected any sort of payment, furthermore, insisting that "a FOKK in need is a FOKK indeed." Access to Death was a perk of membership. Governor Kennedy chatted affably with Cheops via text before asking if Death was available, and Cheops answered "FOKK yeah!"

Death went to pay Cyrus an unofficial visit, but Cyrus learned of Death's approach and ran away to Russia. The savvy Cyrus was well prepared for another murder attempt and had not only bribed someone in Cheops' organization to tip him off but had also identified Russia as a good place to fly under the radar for a while. A little protection money went a long way in Russia, especially with the favorable exchange rate. Hiding overseas was lonely, but he improvised. He didn't dare maintain contact with Goldie via advanced (and traceable) technology but found pleasure in mailing her postcards, which, although they afforded no concealment of contents, had the advantage of being so alien to contemporary experience that no one in the Juckman household even knew what they were and so failed to intercept and read them.

Once again, it fell to Ms. Bonnie to clean up the mess.

Governor Kennedy's attempt at crisis management failed to yield positive results. The attempt to whack Cyrus after tarring him as a seducer by no means quieted things down. By now, the scandal had reached such an intensity that it could no longer be covered up. Not only was the affair too big to be contained, but the moral high ground also proved unattainable, because Morgan wasn't charismatic enough to be accepted in the court of popular opinion as the righteous avenger of his wife's honor and instead appeared to the world as the petty, possessive putz that he was. The immunity once conferred by The Ambassador's reputation had long since expired. King Kong was also getting tired of the Juckmans' shenanigans and was increasingly loath to be involved with them. Something had to be done, some semblance of damage control, to show the world that the Juckman family was at least trying to make itself right. A display of sanity was imperative. Accordingly, it was indispensable that the matriarch take the helm. Though well past sixty years of age, she rose to the challenge.

Bonnie Juckman's first impulse was to annul Goldie's marriage to Morgan Schwartzenberg and to marry her off to someone else. Perhaps some new blood in the family, with a new set of political connections, would turn things around. (Again, Bonnie was just old-fashioned enough to assume that Goldie would have to be married to somebody.) The positives far outweighed the negatives. Morgan would, Bonnie knew, be an easy sacrifice. Everyone wanted him gone. He had brought nothing into the family except shame. Bonnie began rifling through old Park School yearbooks, looking for Jewish names to include on an A list of potential replacement sons-in-law.

She considered, though, that no one besides Morgan could be prevailed upon to excuse Goldie's past behavior. That obstacle—the knowledge that her beloved daughter really wasn't much of a catch anymore— loomed larger and larger in Bonnie's mind until she came to see that Goldie's current dogshit husband remained her best bet. Beggars, after all, couldn't be choosers. Morgan Schwartzenberg's nonexistent bargaining position in family politics had always been his chief virtue. All in all, Bonnie reflected, Morgan would be easier to manage than to replace. Management, after all, was Bonnie's forte. *Better to have him inside the tent pissing out* . . . Here Bonnie's fluency with colorful political verbalisms served her well.

When she heard that Cyrus Schumacher had been driven off, she instructed Goldie not to resume her relations with Morgan. "Stay away from that boy," mother warned daughter, as though protecting her from a mere drive-in movie groper. On this point, Goldie needed no direction, but she had already guessed that her mother would take the long view and ultimately send her back into her ludicrous marriage for strategic reasons. She needed time to recover, anyway.

Bonnie let Morgan stew in suspense for a few weeks before making her move. Her situational grasp had never been firmer. *Timing is essential in politics.* Only after a panic-inducing interval had passed did she open communications. She sent a messenger to summon Morgan, ostensibly to discuss his severance from the family. It was important that Morgan believe that such was the conference's purpose. *Misdirection comes in handy too. Anything that disconcerts him is a good thing.* After waiting so long for the other shoe to drop, Morgan was in a desperate apprehension and Bonnie in a good position to have everything her way. It would be the matriarch's finest hour. She prepared a room for his reception, reeking with Giorgio Armani Acqua di Gioia, to remind him how egregiously he had sinned. Bonnie would turn all his senses against him.

When Morgan arrived, Ms. Bonnie addressed him angrily, enumerating his faults: "You're nothing but an ambulance-chasing gonif. Everybody knows it." (*Okay. So I'm a gonif.* Morgan almost smiled through his terror at this remark, for he'd never aspired to be anything else. *Is that supposed to be an insult?* His eyes now darted in confusion as well as in fright. The butterflies in his stomach flew in all directions.) "A gonif," Bonnie emphasized. The smell of her perfume mixed unpleasantly with the odor of aggressive perspiration, which wafted directly to Morgan's flaring nostrils. She jabbed at his heart with her pointer. Several bracelets jingled and attracted Morgan's attention to the wrinkled flesh on her wrists, removing all doubt that he was in for a dose of primordial, matronly discipline. "That's all you were when you married my daughter; that's all you are now. A *pisher*. A total nothing." She looked at him sideways with one eye, as though focusing her attack. "It's not like we didn't give you a chance. You can't say we held you back; on the contrary. We gave you plenty of chances, along with our daughter. We gave you plenty of time too. Ambassador Schloss and I waited and waited for you to make something of yourself—a judge, full partner, anything— but all you've done is to drag us through one disgrace after another. 'Disappointment' doesn't come close to describing what you are."

She inserted a few tears for effect. Then she resumed her speech, and Morgan sensed that she was approaching the nitty-gritty, in which she would lay down the ground rules for how it was going to be from now on.

"After all the things we've given you—and all the crap you've given us—the least you can do for our family is to donate whatever they need at Park School to finish the Schloss Center. The fundraising's almost done; you go ahead and top it off." (*Huh, will money make it all good? Well, I've got some.* Morgan grasped at the golden straw. His favorite number from the *Cabaret* soundtrack started to play in his mind.) Bonnie was referring to the Ronald A. Schloss Center for Alternative Liberty, which was to be the Brooklandville campus's first skyscraper, intended to house the school's political science department. Once fully erected, it would serve as a towering monument to the instinct for public service that had come to define America's best and brightest.

"Don't get the wrong idea about giving to the Schloss Center," Bonnie continued dishing it out. Morgan tensed up again. "That's what you're going to do for us, not for yourself. I'm not asking you to do it; I'm telling you. It's time to take out your checkbook and start paying your dues." The wise woman knew her son in law and could see that Morgan was already daydreaming of the figure he would cut as a patron of education. Bonnie shook her head. "You're still not getting it. Apparently, you let your little photo op at the King Kong Colosseum go to your head. That's why I'm telling you that you're not the star of the show. Don't start going around like some big shot, just because you're giving Park a pile of money. Your head's too big for the little nebbish that you are. Paying doesn't guarantee playing. Any putz can have money. You're not a big shot." She cleared her throat of phlegm, producing a sound that seemed to lead in to the next blast of Yiddish. "You're not a *shtarker*." Bonnie made sure she was looking down at him. "You're nothing without us. Don't forget it. You're lucky we *let* you into our family." She raised her hand for emphasis. "When they carve your stupid name on the wall of donors, remember that it's our name on the building. That's how you'll tell the difference between big and little. Even if people do recognize your Schwartzenberg on the wall, they'll all know you're just Goldie's husband; and that brings us to . . ." A cloud passed before the sun, and the room got darker.

"We won't even discuss what you tried to do to Goldie. It makes me sick." Ms. Bonnie's gaze was now focused on the bridge of Morgan's nose, sharply enough to cleave off the top of his skull. Again, she let the suspense build. Morgan swallowed hard and nearly forgot to resume breathing. He thought he would black out. The chattering of his teeth was audible.

Bonnie's voice quieted to a whisper. "I just want to say one thing: Since you're the pathetic loser, what are *you* doing trying to get rid of *her*?" Her enunciations rose above the low volume of her voice like punches. "You, a total nothing! And *my daughter* . . ." Bonnie's brow was white-hot with rage. It raised the room temperature by a good three degrees. The air conditioner clicked on. The sound added a base of white noise to Bonnie's accented tirade. "It should be the other way around. You'd better watch yourself. *We* have every reason to get rid of *you*. You think we couldn't? You're hanging by a thread, you know." Some instinct directed her eyes to a shelf of old books, where her American lit anthology from Park yet reposed under decades of dust. "Have you ever read 'Sinners in the Hands of an Angry God'?" Morgan hadn't, but he could grasp the application from the title.

"Goldie can take her pick of better men than you. You think I'd stop her? (And anyone would be better than you. A Calvert Street pimp would have more class.) No one can blame her for trying. Society women have affairs all the time, especially if their husbands are scum. People say, 'You go, girl!' every time she cheats on you. No one takes your side. She doesn't need you for anything, any more than the family does. We Juckmans can do whatever we want. That's the reality, Morgan."

Of course, Bonnie didn't care—nor had she ever cared—about the liberation of the wife as much as she sought to maintain her control over the husband; so she brandished the image of Goldie unleashed, solely as a means of reducing Morgan to a state of beggarly despondency —which tactic soon began producing evident results. Most of Bonnie's diatribe had been punctuated by the sounds of Morgan passing gas, as he had consumed a large quantity of Turkish apricots before the unexpected meeting. Blame college, again, for placing its graduates at a disadvantage. Young Morgan and his chums had used Turkish apricots to fuel farting contests back at Duke, and he'd developed an unfortunate taste for them. Now, finding himself so explosively coming apart at the seams, he slid off his chair in abject defeat and fell with a flatulent flop to the floor.

Morgan hit his head on the floor until he bled. *One hit head, again hit head, three hit head*, he remembered from the subtitles of an old Hong Kong movie; and he seemed to be disintegrating with the effort. Coins spilled out of his pocket. His phone complained, "Ouch, that hurt, you fuckin' jerk," in Porky Pig's voice, as he'd programmed it to do if it were ever jostled or thumped. Farts blasted from his ass with each impact of his forehead. Having hit the rock bottom of humiliation, he turned naturally to a higher power. He rose to his knees and implored the Almighty to forgive him. He began speaking in tongues. He beat himself with both hands. He kissed Bonnie's foot. He tore out tufts of his hair. He drooled. He whimpered. He vomited. He farted some more. His eyes rolled. Tears flooded his face. A stalactite of mucus dangled from his nose. He searched all around for aid. He felt for the mezuzah he used to wear around his neck when he was a child. Instinctively, he called for his wife. *My wife—do I still have a wife?* "Goldie!" his hoarse voice was barely audible. Light from the main globe of the chandelier refracted through his tears, appearing to him as dagger-like rainbows and making him feel that he was drowning, sending a fresh cascade of snot pouring out of his schnoz.

Thereupon, Ms. Bonnie said, "You're nothing but a weakling. Jesus! wipe your nose already." She regarded him with narrowed eyes as he swayed on his knees for a few more moments. She produced a used Kleenex from the sleeve of her sweater and handed it to him. "The conspiracy against my Goldie you couldn't possibly have managed yourself. You're not that clever. Someone must have used you." As Morgan used the Kleenex to de-snotify himself, Bonnie paused to lower her voice again. "It's Micah who's gotten you involved in all this, isn't it? It was Micah all along, right?" Bonnie tilted her head back to look down her nose at Morgan. He stopped whimpering.

By voicing suspicion of Micah, Bonnie was playing her trump: Though watchful of her son, she was not so obsessed that she really believed Micah to have been involved in the plot against Goldie; she was giving Morgan an opening and hoping he took it. *Yes, yes, let's say it was Micah.* Though her son in law was nearly crazed with panic, in his desperation he perceived the fly-fishing filament of a lifeline. Bonnie noticed his beady eyes darting around more than usual, as he considered all the angles; then they settled down, as though he'd made up his mind.

Morgan looked up and assented to her allegation. By now, his nuzz had been wiped and the Kleenex thrown away. He nodded tremulously as though genuflecting. He smiled sheepishly. Bonnie really had no need to be crafty, for Morgan would have agreed to anything. Pinning it all on Micah would satisfy both parties in the current conference. To Bonnie's shoes he gibbered, "Mm . . . Mm . . . Micah." His heart rate went down and his body relaxed.

Ms. Bonnie said, "You make me sick. Look at you. You probably pissed yourself. For God's sake stop groveling." She motioned for him to get up from the floor and continued to gesture imposingly as she went on. "This is how we'll handle it. Since Micah put you up to everything, you're not even important enough to punish; even so, the idea of having you around anymore is so nauseating, I'll need some time with it. Just like you need some time in the doghouse. You may not have my daughter back now. Things aren't reverting to normal just yet. Don't even think of it." She shook her head. "You don't deserve her. Jesus Christ!" She waved her hand to dissipate Morgan's flatulence. The gesture encompassed Morgan himself in the general noxiousness. "Only when the memory of the injury you dealt to her is erased will I again consider her your wife. In the meantime, stew in it." The air conditioning clicked off. A creaking sound continued for a few seconds, as the wood paneling of the room adjusted to the reduced air flow. Morgan settled back into his chair. He felt strangely light. He'd stopped farting.

Although Bonnie had sentenced Morgan only to probation, its length had yet to be determined. She consulted the calendar. Bonnie preferred physical calendars and planners to the ones in her phone, because they harkened back to simpler days when humans were the masters of time, and also because their artistic decoration transcended the little screen, as was the case with her current calendar. It was a give-away from a Chinese restaurant, with a picture of a tiger dressed as an artist marking the current month. He wore a smock and a beret and reminded Bonnie of the old Ambassador in his unworldly complacency. She ran her eyes over it slowly, letting Morgan twist in the wind for a few moments more. The air conditioner clicked on again. The tiger seemed to be waiting for her orders. Although Bonnie would have liked to commune with him a bit longer, her mind returned to the business at hand and she flipped the calendar to the next month, where a human-eyed eagle greeted her with a saucy grin.

She selected a date six weeks in the future as the couple's earliest opportunity to meet again. She flipped the calendar back to the present month. Bonnie nodded once at the tiger, formalizing her decision. *Six weeks ought to give him enough time to count his blessings*, she reflected. Her nose twitched as she looked across at Morgan. *It should also give us enough time to meet with our lawyers.* She opened her mouth with a spittle-laden click of her tongue. She tuned the page of the calendar once more to the eagle month and tapped the designated square with her fingernail. "On this date," she said, "I will send her over to you. Not one minute before." She sniffed. "Use the time well to become a better man. You've got one last chance to behave yourself. Make the most of it. It's better than you deserve." Morgan was listening raptly, and Bonnie pressed her advantage. "You'd better take good care of her this time. Don't forget. We'll be watching you." Bonnie let go of the calendar page and it fell back into place, revealing the current month again. She glanced sideways once more at the tiger before returning her attention to Morgan. *Here it comes.* "Naturally, we'll have a set of conditions for you to follow, if you want to stay in the family. We've every right to impose them. These *conditions* will be put down on paper. You'll agree to them. Never take her for granted. You understand? Never take us for granted. We're up here and you're down there. What we giveth, we can taketh away. That's all." She turned away from Morgan, signaling that their conversation was over. It took Morgan a while to realize that he'd been dismissed.

Morgan could not believe his good fortune at finding the path to forgiveness so open. Bonnie had subjected him to a wrenching ordeal, but if he understood the bottom line correctly, he was going to be okay. He rose from his seat, a little dizzy. He regained awareness of his body. He realized he was drenched in sweat and stank horrifically. *That's the smell of terror and Turkish apricots.* It was nearly enough to knock him back down. Staggering, he maintained his footing as he peeled his damp underpants away from his ass. He promised to comply with Ms. Bonnie's injunctions and then returned home. He'd never been so happy to be driving away from anywhere. The trip back to his (and Goldie's) house on Velvet Ridge Drive took less than five minutes. It was enough time for the smell of his car to overcome the stench of his body, and he yearned even more for the odors of his own abode. He was whistling by the time he got there. The *Pink Flamingoes* Semicentennial pink flamingoes on his front lawn gleamed in supernatural ecstasy. Alighting from his LEAF, he took a deep draft of the sparkling suburban air. It filled his lungs with hope for a new life. He was in better spirits than he usually was. (With the sensibility of a paramecium, he'd always been content enough, but now, having expected to lose everything and receiving instead a light punishment, he was ready to appreciate the miraculous nature of his own favored existence.) Maybe there really was a God, making His power known by allowing good things to happen to bad people. "For if every sin were now visited with manifest punishment, nothing would seem to be reserved for the final judgement." A self-inflicted blow that should have been fatal had resulted in nothing more than sweat-stained clothes and dirty underwear. Thus was Morgan Schwartzenberg humbled.

Now Morgan stripped and showered. Refreshed, he sat before the picture window in the kitchen, watching young cardinals flutter through the forsythia in the back yard. Max-Norm Aire-Girotua rushed over to ask what had happened, but Morgan ignored him. He didn't want to think about what he'd tried to do. He didn't feel like talking. Max-Norm, not into birdwatching, grew bored and left. It was mid-morning, as good a time as any to turn over a new leaf. Morgan was now amply supplied with both hope and horror. The sun streamed through the kitchen skylight, thrilling Morgan with life's restored potential but also revealing the filth that needed cleansing. It showed him how he should apply himself.

Morgan put his house in order. He was not going to let his suspended sentence go to waste. Over the next few days, he was a model of serene obsession. His only thought was of redemption. He threw away old beer bottles and pizza boxes. He cleaned the windows. He cleaned the carpets. The bullfight posters went. He smoothed every quilt and coverlet on every bed and mattress, in preparation for his second chance at marriage. He installed a mirror for the bedroom ceiling. He tested and sanitized every dildo and vibrator. Anything that could possibly make Goldie happy became a priority. Most of the housecleaning he did on his own, as a sort of penance. He whistled while he worked. Days turned to weeks. He was sensitive to every piece of lint that fell to the immaculate floor, and he vacuumed it up promptly. The members of his household marveled at his reformed behavior. They sang the praises of his cleanliness. (And they were glad that they hardly had to do any work. After the first week or so, he didn't even ask them where anything was.) They wondered at its cause. Like all domestics, Morgan's household staff were well attuned to family politics. It was no mystery that Goldie was coming back, for Morgan made no secret of the impending reunion; but it was impossible to account for the reconciliation. Most knew what he'd planned to do to his wife. None could guess at what had passed between him and his mother in law. "She must have something up her sleeve. Why would Ms. Bonnie go easy on him?" they puzzled. "And who's this new Morgan who came skipping out of the main house that day?" Whatever had wrought the change, though, they were grateful for it. Morgan was nicer to them. Morgan even smelled better.

And so, the unhappy couple got back together.

On the appointed day, Goldie returned to her matrimonial home. What could have been going through her mind? Initially resentful that Bonnie would even consider sending her back to Morgan, she happily acceded once Bonnie acquainted her with the *conditions* that would govern her restored marriage; and so she choreographed her retrocession as a triumphal march. There was to be no intimation that she was going begging back to Morgan. It was all-important, she knew, to make the right impression. Attitude was of the essence. Naturally, she contrived to be about forty minutes late. (Making Morgan wait was a stratagem that came naturally both to Goldie and to Bonnie.) She arrived in a limousine once used by her father, which bore the Department of Education's official seal. It nosed slowly up the driveway, its tinted windows keeping Goldie seductively hidden for as long as possible. She ordered the dancing car hydraulics to be activated. A brief automotive breakdance ensued and then, the point being made, the bucking subsided and the car came to a halt next to the pink flamingoes. The limo's sound system played "Who's Sorry Now?"—neither the Patsy Cline nor the Connie Francis antique but the contemporary bubblecum dance track popularized by the pre-teen girl-power group TCHT! (pronounced "Touch It" but short for "These Cunts Have Teeth") that Goldie loved for its subtlety. The gull-wing door opened, and Marigold Juckman swung her naked legs out—she was "wearing" nothing but a holographic string bikini. Goldie was carried from the chariot by a pair of Maori huntsmen, with each supporting a thigh and a breast on each side. They bore their luscious passenger with a stability that contrasted supernaturally with the pulsing background beat, and Goldie flashed a neon-enhanced smile. Her mother, Ms. Bonnie, walked up the driveway before her. She too glided along, aloof from the noise-track. The matriarch had determined in advance to remain silent and betray no emotion, but she couldn't help singing along to "Who's Sorry Now?" She was old enough to recall earlier versions of the song. She wore, coincidentally, a rhinestone-studded denim dress once owned by Patsy Cline. The scent of Acqua di Gioia accented her presence as well. Her ten-inch heels were stabilized by the latest anti-gravity technology. The fancy footwear added to the sense that she was gliding—in fact she'd turned them to the "glide" setting for the occasion.

All members of the "bridal party" held up their smartphones, which emanated confusing strobe lights. Goldie's virtual bikini began sparkling. The headdresses and grass skirts of the Maori bridebearers were also fitted with flashbulbs, which pulsated to the rhythm of their footfalls. No attempt was made to coordinate the light display, and the effect was of a sci-fi laser battle. Such displays once induced epilepsy, but recent generations had grown used to them. No amount of flashing light could faze America's youth of the twenty-first century. It was a milestone of evolution with no downside save for a permanent bloodshotting of the eyes—which the bride's entourage highlighted for the occasion by means of luminescent contact lenses. The limo started leaping around again, and Goldie's people raised an ululating shriek.

Morgan came out to greet them wearing his interview suit. He wore it on all special occasions (except at the King Kong Coliseum archway dedication, when he'd grudgingly donned the kilt). The survivor of a two-for-one sale at the mall, it was the best outfit Morgan owned. He actually thought it would be enough to impress Goldie, and it was indeed flashy in its own way. It too was replete with rhinestones. However, it lacked all the other spectacular effects that now danced about Goldie, and Morgan felt dreadfully outclassed. Dazzled by the frugging limousine, the hormonally-overloaded soundtrack, the throbbing strobes, and his Maori-fondled wife, Morgan at first stood petrified, but he soon came to his senses, realizing he had a part to play. Boldly he stepped forward. He made to embrace Ms. Bonnie, but she held him off with a smirk. Morgan froze again at this rebuff, returning the initiative to Bonnie. She gestured before and behind. The TCHT! song came to an orgasmic climax, and everyone looked in the directions Bonnie pointed. Two groups of lawyers materialized. One group, who were all women, flocked to Goldie (now dismounted from her Maories); the other, all men, to Morgan. They were conservatively dressed, except for their mirror-plated yarmulkes. Ms. Bonnie nodded, and the bridesmaids and bridegrooms of the law proceeded to finalize the *conditions* of the restored union. They exchanged a backdated prenuptial agreement, which Morgan promised never to violate. The flummoxed Morgan was made to understand that his mere signature would not be enough, and he knew what he was being required to do. With his dagger, he nicked his thumb and applied his bloody print to the last page of the document. Goldie now turned toward the house, at no point having looked at Morgan. The lawyers vanished. The limo stopped shimmying and drove away, taking the music with it. The guests traipsed inside. Morgan, alone, wandered in after them.

In celebration, everyone drank and made merry all through the night. (The party lights were visible from space. People moseyed over from neighboring mansions, eager to play a part in the Juckmans' roisterous rededication to normalcy. Many of them paired off and took to the corn maze.) Everyone, that is, except Goldie and Morgan, who retired to the bedroom only to discuss the prenup, especially its copious lifestyle clauses. Morgan, though a lawyer himself, was slow to comprehend the humiliating *conditions* to which he'd assented in blood; so Goldie was obliged to spell it out for him, dispassionately and indeed rather graphically. The party did fine without them. (The party did fine without Morgan, that is, for Goldie soon joined in the frolic.) Each family employee, from the most menial laundress to the highest-ranking massage therapist, ate and drank enough for two. The roast-beef slicer was a busy man that evening. Crates of imported Japanese Zima were consumed. We won't even discuss the stuffed mushroom caps. Ruckleshaus Schumacher contributed some real crab cakes, which were the most popular items on the buffet table. Good old cousin Ruckleshaus, as usual, took care of everything. Fish and Wildlife agents, as well as the fire marshal, were paid off.

Max-Norm changed his patron, and Micah changed his line of attack.

Max-Norm Aire-Girotua, Morgan's servant and instigator, found his position growing ever less promising. The more he pondered his situation, the more he came to feel sorry for himself. True, he'd gotten away with attempted murder, and he was pleased enough to have avoided paying the death penalty on live television, but now that the danger had passed, wasn't it time to start going places again? Max-Norm had always aimed high. He'd assumed his employer to be a rising star, FOKK that he was, but now the spunk seemed to have left him. Was Morgan just going to give up? Max-Norm gradually woke to the reality that he'd bet on a loser. It was time to switch horses—in mid-stream, if necessary. As Morgan had submitted so abjectly to his mother in law, the ambitious Aire-Girotua transferred to Micah Juckman's camp.

He took to his new friends immediately. *Micah's a creep with class*, Max-Norm berated himself. Making up for lost time with an *I shoulda started hanging out with Micah a long time ago*, Max-Norm began to offer Micah pointers on how to increase his online presence ("There's a lotta attention waiting out there on Goodreads for whoever sets up a Hungarian Literature in Translation group," he promised), and Micah came to view him as eminently clever. Soon, Max-Norm was Micah's right-hand man—not literally, of course, for the seating arrangement in the Federal Hill jacuzzi tended to be boy-girl-boy-girl. (The earlier ostracism had passed. Micah had attracted a new generation of groupies.) He waited patiently for Micah's next move in the Juckman civil war and for whatever orders Micah might give him when the time came.

For his part, Micah perceived that there was now even less hope of alienating his sister from his mother. The two were cooperating as tightly as ever, and this latest project of theirs affected Micah in an especially tender area. *I can't believe Goldie went quietly when Mom sent her back to Morgan*, he obsessed. It was galling enough that Bonnie was playing the part of the pimp—twice now for the sake of the same unworthy lout—and Goldie so brazenly betraying their childhood bond; but what made it worse was the knowledge that his mother's sole interest in the sordid farce was, as usual, political. To him, the matriarch's elaborate charade for the sake of Goldie's "re-spectability" felt like a reassertion of control over both Goldie and the family in general. *Am I wrong to think it's time for her to step aside? Why does everyone keep listening to the old bat? They should be listening to me.* Since he still refused to submit to Ms. Bonnie's authority, he believed he had no choice but to consider Goldie, likewise, an enemy. Reconciliation was now out of the question. Micah's logic was biblical: If Goldie wasn't with him, then she was against him. Micah's pretentions to family leadership notwithstanding, his chief motivation (for Micah was sticking to type as much as his mother) was to cause pain; only this time, he would serve it up in a different form. *OK*, he pouted to no one, *you can keep your respectability, and I'll keep your money. See how you like that.* Dollar signs lit up in Micah's eyes, as he schemed to inflict a monetized punishment. He would aim the blow directly at his big sister.

Thereupon, Micah intrigued for Goldie to be cut off from the family and left to her fate as Morgan's wife. The details absorbed a good amount of his excess energy. Taking an uncharacteristic interest in the family business, Micah found that The Ambassador had left a lot of power in his eldest son's hands, clearing the way for this assertion of financial control. It made Micah feel that his father was smiling down on him, even as he sought to punish his sister. "With such a capable provider, she won't need anything from us anymore," he sneered to his lawyer, as he planned his coup. "Let's hear it for Ms. Bonnie the management guru, for knowing how to pick dependable people. If Mom thinks Morgan is such a wonderful husband, then he should be wonderful enough to take care of his wife. Mom made Goldie's bed," he continued to rant, ignorant of the *conditions* of his sister's restored marriage, "and now Goldie will have to sleep in it."

He stated his purpose at the annual shareholders' meeting, where the entire clan was assembled. (Micah left his lawyer out of it, with a testosterone-laden "I've got this," as he wanted all of the spotlight for himself.) The gathering took place in the restored living room of Juckman Manor, and Micah's smile, which he copied from his own bar mitzvah photo, once more adorning the wall, lulled the family into a false sense of security. Micah whipped out the papers as soon as the meeting began, not waiting for the "new business" segment of the agenda. All were taken by surprise, disconcerting resistance. Even Bonnie was unprepared and could only stare straight ahead in silent fury. Micah continued to beam with pubescent pride through the dropping of his bombshell. "Does anyone have any questions?" he hissed, when he was done.

Among his brothers, only one, Jeremy, objected. "Remember," he said softly, playing the role of peacemaker, "we're brothers and sisters, not just shareholders." Stopping Morgan's allowance made sense, he admitted, but Goldie was flesh and blood. "Let's not forget either," he went on, "that Goldie has been the victim in all this." Jeremy promised to hire a few lawyers of his own, and Micah's spiteful campaign was thus bogged down. The two brothers eyed each other coolly, while everyone else looked left and right and stuttered their incredulity. The board meeting dissolved in acrimony. And that was it: The Juckman family never convened again for business or pleasure.

That evening, Goldie texted Jeremy: "ttly FUCKED. NOW of all times! just bought new car! with all options—even seat warmer witch make me feel like just crapped in pants but dint want to be cheep. Cant belief micah did that. after all i do for him. why he say shit abt me? 😞 like IM a slut?! BS! WTF. who he think he is?" (Micah had impugned Goldie's chastity, in his argument for withdrawing her support.) "ayatola micah. in this day an age. well fukkit. rather be dead then live wit slut shame. . . . but still crazy angry at micah. feel like punch in face. still shaking. in front of everybody! right in family room. my own brother. now i wake up and smell bs. 'family is forever. count on each other. flesh n blood. you n me against world. always have your back. juckman strong. here 4 u. your safe at home' YEAH, RIGHT. give me break. ttl bs. now I know. family run like rats (except u). u not like micah. *Low battery power.* shit, hafta plugin soon. not even mom saw this coming. still trust her because no choice and she get me good deal with morgan, but seriously? just sit there. feel sorry for her. maybe shes get old. actually we all just sit there. brb." Goldie plugged in her phone and went to the kitchen for a glass of acai juice before getting back to her texting and venting.

"like mica never fool around! pot calling kettle black. micah, u no? he the slut. he fool around with kids. young ones. bimbo girlz. in jacuzzi. sometimes fool around wit ME! he still always want to. like old days. every time n place. not just in shower, you know. everone know. rumors true."

Goldie got in bed (the charger cord was long enough) and kept thumb-typing. "im good sister, let him do what he want. his choice. lot of stuff. you name it. even titty fuck. that his favorite. he get out of system. I thought was helping. always look out for him. my job. big sister. want to be good big sister. since we were kids. was nice to be there for him. been thru many thing together. esp dad die n things get crazy after that.

"now hes out of control. must be paranoid. why defund me? what I do wrong? too much love for him. he attack close people. crazy. like baby. he shuld know I was only 1 on his side. thick n thin. in his corner. worry about him. ALWAYS. fix polit situation for him. kiss cheops for him. make it safe for him to come home. who protrect him now????"

Goldie sat up in bed. "not care. I not fix it. not my job anymore. thankless task. he ruin family. nothing left to fix. ne way thanx you nice to stick up for me. maybe can pick up pieces, just no micah. ❤ xoxo." Goldie put the phone on do not disturb, switched off the light, and went to sleep.

It's possible, though unlikely, that one could find a comparable example of such abject supplication, so unrestrainedly did she thank Jeremy for his support. The confessional nature of her missive suggested desperate gratitude, but Goldie was not unaware of the effect that the TMI would have on her defender. Her sharing of confidences was most moving. Such a set of intimate details can only invite the interlocutor into the sharer's world. It made Jeremy, who always tried to be a decent person, feel that he'd been right to challenge Micah. (He and Micah were cordial enough, but he'd never been admitted to Micah's inner circle of playmates.) In fact, Jeremy appeared to himself like a knight in shining armor protecting the fayre damsel Goldie. Thus was the good brother encouraged to do the right thing.

However, her text was as exquisitely crafted—and calculated— as anything she ever wrote. The prolonged chat might have seen the transition from the old sweet Goldie to the new clever one. The fayre damsel was a player. Of course, she was the target both of Morgan's murderous plot and now of Micah's attempt to cut her off, but the long lament about her unrequited nurturing of Micah was mostly a performance designed to make Jeremy weigh in on behalf of her material interests. As unaffectedly as Goldie had expressed her hurt and resentment, she was at this point chiefly interested in maintaining a style of life that required a great deal of money. No other type of fulfilment had panned out for her. Goldie's eyes were filled with dollar signs too, although in a certain light they looked like hearts.

Micah's low road led lower and lower, until he was lost in the swamp.

For the time being, Micah maintained cordial relations with both his mother and with Ruckleshaus Schumacher to ensure that they refrained from open hostility. Perhaps, as his mother's son, he sought to *manage* the situation. He could be pragmatic when he wanted to be. Furthermore, Micah was by nature passive-aggressive: He excelled at chipping away at someone else's stable situation, but he navigated poorly in chaos. The lawsuit was between him and Jeremy, and Bonnie and Ruckleshaus seemed disinclined to get involved. They were going to let the lawyers deal with it. That was fine with him. The situation remained stable, and he was on track to dominate it intact.

As strong as his position seemed to be, though, he was apprehensive of a sudden turn of the tide against him. Paranoia was creeping into his persona. *A wise man plans for the worst, even while hoping for the best*, Micah remembered reading in a fortune cookie. What concerned him was his big sister. Goldie had yet to be neutralized, and his fear that Bonnie would use her as a weapon against him remained paramount. Such an eventuality would be unprecedented, and in the war of hurt that he'd been waging with his mother, which he'd started by turning her brother against her, it would count as an unanswerable payback. What he dreaded most, in other words, far more than a financial or political setback, was a shock to his intimate psyche, of the kind that could only come via Goldie. He'd been hurt by Goldie before, but never with her intent; if now she were to play an active part in some humiliation staged by Bonnie, it would wreck him, and to avoid the blow he felt to be coming, he was prepared to do anything to anticipate it.

One day, he huddled with Missy (the sister with whom he had once quarreled over her personal assistant, Riggi) and Max-Norm Aire-Girotua. Spring was again in the air, bringing with it the cocktail of pollen and hormones that has always inflamed and incited homo sapiens in high school and beyond. It was time to feel things out. No food was served; all was business. The meeting took place in Micah's Federal Hill jacuzzi. Its jets were turned up to full blast. Missy sat between Micah and Max-Norm, the better for everyone to feel things out. Micah knew who he was dealing with: Missy had always been the most susceptible to feelings of sibling rivalry, which

Micah could easily turn from himself to Goldie; and Max-Norm would do whatever Micah wanted him to, the bolder the better. The scheme they hatched was grandiose. Jacuzzi-born schemes usually are, and the plotters had an antecedent to build upon. Each felt that he or she could manage anything better than Morgan could. As a matter of pride, they all vied to one-up Morgan, even in the realm of murder. This time there would be no holding back. The adults were running things now. They'd show Morgan how it was done. Goldie would be taken out.

The plot would hinge on two other people. (*All right! this is what you call brainstorming.* Micah dibbled a little cocoanut mango oil into the churning bath water, to stimulate creativity. *Now that we've got our thinking caps on, we'll be able to work out something foulproof* [In this mental aside, Micah meant *foolproof*; he was laxadaisical about precision.]) Although it's rarely a good idea to bring others into a murder conspiracy, in this case, a couple of extra players were needed to gain access to protected areas. Micah, after all, had long ago lost *access* to Goldie, and thus the cabal required co-conspirators still possessing an in. Such helpers needed to be recruited strategically. What kind of person held Goldie's trust but could be moved—or tricked—into betraying it? One was Ambassador Schloss's youngest daughter, Zoey. (Her real name was Bethany, but she'd changed it to avoid the embarrassing initials—an option that Bonnie was too stubborn to utilize, although a similar logic might explain why the matriarch didn't take her husband's last name.) She was a natural choice. *Rebel Without a Cause* might as well have been written for her, and she was in fact a fan of a recent musical version, in which Jim massacres the entire LAPD while singing "I've Got the Bullets!" Zoey liked to chart her own course and was the only Juckman never to attend college. She'd not so much as applied. (Even The Ambassador, despite his position in the education establishment, had grown tired of the old racket by the time Zoey became eligible. "Maybe college is a little overrated," he'd admitted to her with a sigh.) She was alert and skilled at Tetris. She'd invented a new generation of touchscreen technology for a virtual cunnilingus app and never accepted a penny for it, calling royalties "bourgeois pimp money." She'd never read a book. She could stick her tongue halfway up each nostril. Owing to her age, Zoey possessed scant memories of the family's earlier ascendency under Ms. Bonnie's discipline and had known only squabbling and dissipation. None of it fazed her. Intrigue and betrayal were common elements of her landscape. In truth, she thought they were normal. She was also a lot like Micah in temperament. Their affinity was obvious from the fact that they both liked watching live animals being eaten on "exotic foods" TV shows. Their age difference, however, had largely precluded their hanging out. For the most part, Zoey was content to admire Micah from a distance. A libertine in her brother's mold, she would be quite pleased to have Goldie cut off (or otherwise out of the picture), leaving more money for her own entertainment budget. The latter was of some importance to Zoey, contempt for bourgeois values notwithstanding. Some of Zoey's entertainment budget, furthermore, was pharmacological.

Zoey, therefore, was one of the new conspiracy's inside operators. The other was the wife of Rusty Khan, the sporting goods distributor who'd programmed Micah's golf caddies. Micah had hired Rusty after acquiring the late Ambassador's massive collection of gold clubs, gifts from foreign dignitaries. He'd done such a fine job that Micah barely had to think about his game at all, leaving his mind free for musing and machination. In fact, Rusty and Micah went way back.

Rusty Khan was Micah's classmate from grade school, valued for his indifference to other people's business. Despite his elite Park School education, Rusty remained content to let others make the world a better place while he concentrated on helping them play a better game of golf. His wife was the former Libby Levin, another grade school classmate. Like her husband, Libby also relished the role of support staff for Baltimore's elite, applying her talents to the kitchen and to the recital hall. Libby Levin-Khan was a cake chef and part-time soprano for the Baltimore Opera. The professional doubling worked well for her, because she could practice her choruses and arias while she whipped up her delectable batters and icings. She often regaled Rusty with the Doll Song from Offenbach's "Tales of Hoffman" because it was easy for him to relate to. (In fact, it was a little *too* easy for him to relate to, for he sometimes crushed on the female caddies he created.) Given the *very* part-time nature of her work with the Baltimore Opera, whose schedule was so frequently disrupted by rioting, it was a good thing she had the cake business. She called it "Got to Gâteau," and she boasted an impressive clientele drawn from the greater Baltimore-Washington area. Her signature creation was a fallen soufflé cake in the shape of the US Capitol, which proved popular among the rulemakers of DC's executive agencies, who, upon helping themselves to a slice, would call it a "sub-delegation."

Even without her husband's connection to Micah, Libby would certainly have become caker to the Juckmans (who would not have wanted to appear to have missed the boat on the most highly-demanded desserts in the mid-Atlantic states); but with her husband's connection, she was nearly a part of the family. Every day found her moving freely between Micah's house and those of his sisters, where she was intimate with everyone, often drinking and singing karaoke with them. Gatherings seemed incomplete without her. Her talent as vocalist made her indispensably welcome, even though she didn't strip when she sang. She was that good. Her rendition of "MacArthur Park" invariably brought tears to every eye. Party guests stopped eating and drinking and elevator-pitching whenever Libby cleared her throat. "I'll never have that recipe again" always resonated with everybody. She was usually held over whenever she wanted to go home, just for a few more songs. None was guarded against her. She knew the lock combinations to all the Juckmans' front doors and their back doors too. This ease of coming and going rendered her indispensable to the conspirators. When Micah proposed making use of her, a weighty silence gave consent.

Of course, Libby Levin-Khan was no murderer, but she could perhaps be duped into playing a supporting role in the crime. Her very sweetness suggested the possibility. An eagerness to please as strong as Libby's has always recommended itself to assholes. Make no mistake, the characters gathered in the jacuzzi that spring day were assholes. As Micah remarked to his co-conspirators, Missy and Max-Norm Aire-Girotua, "We can't count Mom out of the game as long as Goldie's still around." He sniffed. A police car siren blared from somewhere across the harbor. "That's why Goldie has got to go." Someone's ass shifted in its plastic seat, producing an underwater farting sound. Missy noticed that Micah was blinking rapidly. He wiped his eyes as he concluded. "Libby Levin is our best chance to get rid of Goldie." The others, again, had been okay with the idea of taking advantage of Libby as soon as Micah broached it and didn't need to hear his rationale. Neither Missy nor Max-Norm really cared about the details. Missy just wanted Goldie out of the way, and Max-Norm just wanted action; in any event, the hot-tub meeting adjourned.

Micah began engaging Libby more frequently in small talk, inserting requests for favors such as reporting how Goldie looked or what she said. Libby, suspecting nothing more than chattiness, happily obliged. Soon, Micah's questions began to focus on Goldie's daily and hourly movements. Were they routine enough to be predicted? Micah enticed Libby with promises of great rewards. To him it was all an investment. A ski weekend in Aspen was a small price for Micah to pay for information about where Goldie took her lunch. "My mom always liked to know what we were up to, and it was nice to know that she cared; but now I'm afraid she's getting too old, so I feel I have to step up for her. It's better for everybody if I know what's going on in the family," he assured her. "If Goldie is acting strangely, for example, it might mean that she's in trouble, and maybe she'd be too proud to ask for help. Why don't you and Rusty stay in Aspen for the whole week? Just let me know where Goldie works out, where she gets her hair done, stuff like that." Libby couldn't resist. It was actually rather touching for her. Micah seemed so concerned for his sister. People said he was creepy, but Libby was pleased to think she knew the truth about him. Besides, she liked to help and enjoyed feeling important. Doesn't everybody—the latter at least? Indeed, she was important, just not in the way she imagined.

As the spring grew greener, the plot ripened apace. Micah knew how keenly Max-Norm Aire-Girotua wished to kill Goldie, and so it was easy to make him a co-conspirator. Max-Norm regretted how, during the previous attack, he'd been shy with Goldie, even while beating her, and the fact of her sexual power over him made him more desperate than ever to squelch it at the source. (During the brainstorming in the hot tub, neither the boy-girl seating arrangement nor the agitated condition of the water prevented Micah from noticing Max-Norm's rising enthusiasm. Micah was jealous, but he knew that he could exploit Max-Norm's perverseness as easily as Libby's kindness.) In fact, each obsessed man tried to outdo the other in eagerness to eliminate his obsession. As planning continued, each displayed his peculiar shade of rottenness. The more Micah worked through the operational details of killing Goldie, the more Max-Norm fantasized, out loud, about the physical ones. Micah and Max-Norm constituted the brains and balls of the operation.

And so the alliance was formally struck. The planning phase was over. It was, Micah intuited, time to put up or shut up, as far as the long-contemplated enterprise was concerned. The essential task was to shore up the organization. Sex and money were the cements that held it together. Nothing else, in Micah's view, kept people on board for the long haul. ("*Sex and money, sex and money,*" in Frank Sinatra's voice, was how Micah liked to spoof the old song "Love and Marriage." It used to make Goldie laugh, but she never realized that Micah wasn't kidding.) Micah sent his god-daughter Calleigh Yentz to Aire-Girotua's bedchamber and promised Libby Levin a hundred thousand dollars, although only three thousand dollars was ever actually given to her. Using sex to secure Max-Norm's commitment was an obvious move, but would money do the trick for Libby? Micah wanted Libby to be financially committed—as well as compromised—in case the shit hit the fan. Although Micah feared that Libby might be too squeamish to allow an unearned wad of cash into her pocketbook, he was able to use her unguardedness and her cultivated naïveté to present himself as someone trying to teach her how the real world worked. Libby's payment was described as a general retainer for making herself useful. "It's no more than you deserve," Micah assured her, "and you shouldn't cheat yourself out of it." Flattered and unsuspecting, Libby accepted with a smile. Thus was she hooked.

The arrangements were finalized during a Spanish dinner at Tio Pepe's downtown. Having Libby present while the foul flow-chart was revealed was yet another means to entangle her. Micah, Missy, Zoey, and Max-Norm spoke elliptically, so that Libby never grasped what was being discussed. Of course, Micah offered to pay for her meal, and she ordered the Zarzuela de Mariscos Costa Brava. Micah had the Mero al Horno. Missy and Zoey split the Paella a la Valenciana, which at any rate was para dos. Max-Norm had a hamburger.

In spite of the intricate plan made on her behalf, Goldie would not keep still.

Goldie and her husband Morgan, as part of the arrangement by which they'd resolved their recent impasse, had pledged not to interfere in each other's affairs. In fact, they scarcely had to speak to one another. Such were the lifestyle clauses. (We've referred to them as *conditions* above, and they were included in the backdated prenup, signed on the occasion of Goldie's grand return home.) The system worked greatly to Goldie's benefit. It was high time, she considered, that something did. She wasted no time exploiting it. Of course, Goldie had been doing pretty much whatever she'd wanted to do for some time, but now Morgan had signed off on it, and so Goldie felt at even greater liberty than before; she was almost glad that Morgan had tried to kill her.

In the late spring, Goldie chartered a yacht and sailed down the Chesapeake Bay to the Hampton Roads area, where her cousin and lover, Cyrus Schumacher, was rumored to be in hiding, after returning from Russia. Supposedly, Cyrus was hanging out on a houseboat down there. It was exhilarating for the goose to hunt for the gander. *Think of the joy that will ensue*, Goldie mused, *when the hunt is successful.* Goldie looked and felt every inch the explorer, poring over maps in the yacht's bridge, questing for her own elusive Seven Cities. She wore a blue and white striped mariniere and a bandana around her neck, and the salty breeze rippled both beautifully.

However, her quarry proved to be quite elusive indeed. Goldie began drumming her fingertips on the helm, as she tacked and turned. She searched from Yorktown to Virginia Beach but searched in vain. The air grew still and sultry, forcing Goldie to employ the motor, which tinged the air with the smell of gasoline. The skies, and Goldie's brow, soon turned cloudy. *Where could he be?* Not even the most cutting-edge Chinese police technology could help her pinpoint Cyrus's whereabouts, for the latter had covered his tracks with the latest Russian camouflage software. Goldie's quandary resembled the paradox of the all-piercing spear and the impenetrable shield, but the shield was winning. After a few weeks, even the ever-hopeful Goldie was thinking of calling it quits. *I don't want to have to look all up and down the Intracoastal Waterway*, she pouted.

As it turned out, Cyrus was living aboard his sailboat, *Cy's Size*, tied up at the Tidewater Yacht Marina in Portsmouth. He'd grown addicted to the (imitation) crab cakes they have there at the dockside restaurant. Despite its impressive name, *Cy's Size* measured only nineteen feet in length. It was made for inconspicuousness. The vessel had been purchased with cash and stripped of any navigational equipment that would leave a signature. Goldie never would have found it by the method she was using. It was luck, then, rather than

Goldie's detective work, that led her to her man. Concerned at the encroaching flabbiness of seaborne life, Goldie had tied up at the marina and started working out at a Portsmouth gym. The lovers were reunited by chance at the Commodore Theatre, where they'd both gone to see *Star Wars XLVII: The Rise of Porkins*. It was a double coincidence. Not only were they taking in the same movie, but they were also ordering mackerel-flavored popcorn, a shared favorite, at the same time, and they heard each other through the darkness phoning in their orders. (The Commodore is a dinner theater.) Thus did fate play its part. Reunited, they moved their seats from the dining area to the balcony, where they could sit in closer proximity. Goldie and Cyrus kissed passionately, dislodging globs of mackerel powder from their lips (each had already gone through a bucket). They were too involved with each other to stand up for the national anthem, but of course, once the feature started, they were mesmerized.

Goldie joined Cyrus on his boat, and together, they set it rocking. "Cover me, Porkins!" was never demanded with greater urgency. Goldie off-hired her yacht and began cruising around with her paramour aboard his cozier and less conspicuous craft. With no particular place to go, they went many places. *Cy's Size* made its presence felt throughout the Tidewater area, as Goldie and Cyrus churned up the Chesapeake estuary. Both had turned off their phones, of course, and the sense of respite from system updates and news feeds was idyllic. Playing at pirates, they "raided" coastal towns—which meant dining at the restaurants there—and rarely stayed in one place for long. When they tired of restaurants, they bought local seafood to eat on the boat, and they never stayed at hotels, preferring to cram themselves into the cramped stateroom each night, which wasn't very comfortable for sleeping, but neither was primarily interested in sleep. They made ripples in this way for over a month. Zeus, or Eros, provided them with good weather. It was never stormy or choppy, and they always had favorable winds. The latter filled their sail and kept the air nice and dry. Presently, they sailed up the Rappahannock River and dropped anchor at Tappahannock. The combination of the waterway's and the town's name held great poetic potential. Riffing off the paired Algonquin words made Goldie and Cyrus even giddier than they'd been. Whenever they weren't fucking, they were rhyming, and sometimes they were doing both. They made up a song, "Cy's Sighs," to immortalize their time together. It was really a hoot.

> Tappahannock on the Rappahannock!
> *Sounds just like a film by Zanuck.*
> *Fuck me manic—Oh God!*
> *Swing my hammock—Oh God!*

They were very happy. Wouldn't you be?
Goldie took a long time returning home.

Our plot returns from the swivers to the connivers.

Back in Baltimore, meanwhile, the days and weeks hung heavy. Truth be told, days and weeks in Baltimore often hang heavy, even for good people not intent on murder. Within Micah's cabal, nerves were at hair-trigger tension all summer, in anticipation of Goldie's reappearance. "Nothing is worse than having an itch you can never scratch." The stressful expectancy could only keep building, the longer Goldie stayed away. (And Goldie stayed away: Even after exhausting the rhyming possibilities of Tappahannock and Rappahannock, her recollection of how the locals pronounced "Norfolk" became sufficient reason for her and her cousin to put in there for a while—"Aw, fuck! why not fuck in Norfolk?" they giggled.) As a result, the plot against her came close to unravelling. Her would-be murderers were not sleeping well. The unease at being "up to no good" can only deepen if one is "up" all night. The conspirators were on the verge of panic.

The first shade of panic was green. The allocation of money to any enterprise, legitimate or criminal, binds the, ah, entrepreneur to it in such a way as to reduce him to a bundle of nerves. It showed up in the ringleader's face. It was apparent in his voice, high-pitched and breathy. Micah regretted that he had committed so much money to a conspiracy that had yet to bear fruit. For what he was putting up, he expected quick results. *When am I going to see some return on this investment?* he grumbled to himself. *Time is money.* Of course, Micah's concern for money was a distortion of other feelings, but it was all he was able to admit. The expression of moral disquiet as business concern is actually quite common, because the *homme d'affaires* feels more in control of things than the sinner, bundle of nerves notwithstanding. Playing the CFO was easier than looking into his soul. Who would want to look into Micah's soul at this stage, anyway?

He texted Zoey, desiring the return of cash that she had stored at Missy's residence. (Perhaps he should not have put it beyond his own reach in the first place. Micah thought it was safer to keep money away from the people who would be handling it for as long as possible. The use of cash as payment was almost completely unheard of by this time, and Micah didn't want to be caught with any; hence he preferred that others handle it, before its final delivery to Libby Levin-Khan. This indirect method paralleled his convoluted psyche. He was really too clever for his own good. Maybe he was growing distrustful of his two younger sisters and was testing their responsiveness. In any case, he'd made things more complicated than they had to be.)

Zoey thereupon texted Missy, and Missy replied as follows:

"Waiting for Goldie to get back is 🐂💩. Total 🐂💩. Get it? Your smart, right? That means bs. Twiddlin our thums all summer. Timesawastin. Let's stop waitin for her n go lookin for her. Better find out where she is now. U no? While trail still hot. This is Goldie were talk about. Probly not hard to find. Hooking up with guys and attracting attention n such. We shud take the nishyative. Use all r people. Send fat lady to annaplis with some of the money. She know goldie. No prob to find her. Then she tell us n we can getter done."

Missy guessed correctly that Goldie had fled down the Bay. They were sisters, after all. The Juckmans used to sail out of Annapolis in the old days, leaving deep impressions on the children. Of course, Goldie had ventured a bit beyond Annapolis, but it wasn't unreasonable to suppose that she'd pass through there, if she were traipsing about the Bay, adding new memories to old. "She can bribe people for news of Goldie. She not raise suspishin anyway. Fat lady I mean. Other one is flashy. Prob has shown herself at expensive restaurant or hotel. Maybe even penthouse sweet. Goldie I mean. Naturally get attention. When we find out then get her. Send Max-Norm. Take by surprise. Then all over. Good plan? At least somebody thinking. Your welcome." Missy shut off her phone, to be off the grid for fifteen minutes.

By "fat lady," she meant Libby Levin-Khan. The moniker was of recent vintage, coined by the Juckman kids. Calling her "fat lady" leant a certain underworld quality to the siblings' communications. They had never spoken of Libby that way before, but now that they were doing something rotten, it seemed natural that they should employ colorful language. The nickname was a reference to the proverbial singer at the end of the opera, although in Libby's case, the lady wasn't really fat. In fact, she was as petite as she was innocent. Putting her to good use, in any case, made sense. As the most positive person among the Tio Pepe junto, Libby was prepared to make the most cheerful contribution, even though she didn't know what was going on. Zoey conveyed Missy's views back to Micah. *What do they need me to be third wheel for? Monkey in the middle*, she complained to herself about her superfluous role in the chain of communication . . . before something else occurred to her. The thought was unsettling. Zoey realized in the back of her head that her acting as messenger had made her an accessory. She also perceived how Micah was trying to dilute the blame by making the conspiracy larger than it had to be. She erased the conversation from her phone, but she knew she'd crossed the Rubicon. She was now more involved than she would have been had she simply batted around some murderous ideas or handled a little cash.

Micah texted back, "Fkn HATE money sittin round doing nuthin. Cud be having good times with it. Ttl 🐑💩. That means bs. ☹ Let me think. Fine! Sick of waiting, anyway. If Missy think we can put it to use then ok. So it's settled. Do what she say. Let's hope Goldie turn up." He slammed down his phone, cracking its screen. Then he paced around for a while, cursing. Fully aware of the soundness of Missy's plan, he nonetheless played the cartoonish part by acting all primitive and thuggy. "Fuckin' kiddin' me," he huffed to nobody.

Zoey sent off Libby Levin-Khan with cash and instructions. By so doing, she graduated from messenger to dispatcher, but this knowledge of even deeper involvement didn't compel her to act like the stereotypical criminal. In contrast to Don Micah, Zoey took refuge behind a screen of suburban normality. (She'd seen enough suburban normality on TV to enable her to imitate it, although it was foreign to her experience.) She feigned nonchalance for her own sake as well as for Libby's. She invited Libby over, on the pretext of giving her a tube of dual-use vanilla extract cake icing and hand cream, and then asked if she would mind going on a little trip. "You're really sweet to be doing this for us," Zoey trilled, over a cup of coffee. "It's great the way you help out the family. Micah is counting on you." Zoey shook her head and raised her pointer, as she offered a clarification. "We all are. Missy and I are concerned too. Goldie's been gone too long, and we don't want her to get in trouble. At first we thought she might have left the country, but now we figure she's staying somewhere a bit closer to home, someplace more familiar. Why not spend a few days in Annapolis, and keep your eyes open while you enjoy yourself there? It's a family stomping ground. You're bound to find Goldie sooner or later. Whereabouts in Annapolis? You know her tastes. Just follow the Juckman pleasure principle. I bet you'll spot her in an Ethiopian restaurant or someplace like that. Otherwise, maybe you'll catch her shopping for that fishy popcorn she likes; but I'm sure you'll see her." Zoey winked. Libby smiled in happy recollection of Goldie's odd snacking habits. "When you do, let us know, and we'll bring her back into the family again. You know it's where she belongs. You really are a good friend."

Then Zoey handed Libby three thousand dollars in cash, enjoining her once more to "Have a good time."

In the event, Libby Levin-Khan did not have to do any snooping in Annapolis. As it turned out, she never made it to "America's Sailing Capital," where Goldie and Cyrus had indeed put in for some Ethiopian food once or twice, during the euphoric course of their cruise. She never had to leave the Baltimore area, in fact. She'd started to pack and had even bought a UV protection parasol (coincidentally, it was a piece of University of Virginia merch), under which she hoped to hide if she ever did have to tail Goldie; but it was a wasted effort. In spite of her thoughtful preparation—which included making reservations to stay in Horn Point, with many marinas and restaurants nearby—fate intervened to deprive her of her downstate excursion. (Good thing she still had her portable CFAR insurance from when she was single.) It was a shame, because she was looking forward to her trip; but at least she was able to do something for the Juckmans, even though it meant going without the faux she-crab soup at the Sailor Oyster Bar for a while longer.

It was Libby's own heads-up play that made her trip unnecessary. On the afternoon of the day before she was to leave on her mission, she spotted Morgan Schwartzenberg coming out of the LA Fitness in Towson and called out in greeting. She recognized him by his leopard-skin sports bra. In spite of her innocence, Libby knew better than to ask Morgan where his wife was (there must have been some reason why Micah and company hadn't thought of such a simple method), but maybe Morgan would let something slip. He crossed York Road to meet her. It seemed to Libby that Morgan looked inordinately chipper; perhaps he was exhilarated by his workout. Perhaps he was expecting that Libby had an extra cake on hand. Morgan was happy to see Libby, and they embraced.

"Got any cakes?" he asked her straightaway, and when told that she didn't, through barely-concealed disappointment, suggested that she join him, in the hope that she could be induced to bake something later. Suspecting nothing, Morgan took Libby on his Vespa to the rental house off Joppa Road where Goldie was laying low. Libby's heart beat faster, as Morgan supplied the details. The Juckman princess was a few days returned to familiar surroundings and was recovering from and ruminating upon her exertions at Tappahannock and other Edens of estuarial ecstasy. Morgan's narration was matter-of-fact. Evidently, Goldie was on the lam from her mother and brother but not from her cuckolded husband, who, with Libby, was greeted warmly at the door by Goldie herself as soon as they knocked. *I guess Morgan is happy as long as he's able to smell her*, Libby speculated as she was released from Goldie's perfumed embrace and took in the smartly-accoutered digs, where a party of about twenty young people was in progress. The atmosphere was as friendly as ever, as though Goldie had never been absent. Libby recognized a face or two, but most of the guests seemed to be new acquaintances, neighbors or even people jogging or walking by, attracted by the sounds of the beat box and persuaded to stay by the ravishing and gregarious Goldie. They joined in a marathon game of Wii bowling, in which Goldie almost always scored in the high 200s. She blushed to applause whenever she notched a strike or picked up a spare. Alexa spun up some beach music. The center of the living room was cleared for dancing, just the circular, friendly kind, with no need for a partner. Goldie wore a sundress, and Libby had never seen her more vibrant. She danced by everyone, beaming and making sure she learned his or her name. The party continued into the night.

It happened early the next morning.

After many hours, Libby rose to leave. She'd been having a fine time, and yes at one point she did feel compelled to slip into the kitchen to whip up a quick strawberry Pocky stick cake, which everyone devoured and which Goldie kissed her for, but now she remembered what she was supposed to be doing. It was past ten o'clock. She'd been there since after lunch. Her eyes were blurry from the video gaming, she said, and the spicy pad thai dinner had disagreed with her. For emphasis, she rubbed her stomach, but so unaccustomed to lying was she, even in gesture, that she confusedly made the sign for "yummy;" yet the upshot was that it was time for her to head home. She pulled out her phone, ostensibly to summon a ride. As she looked for Max-Norm's number among her contacts—she had not yet put it on her speed-dial—she moved toward the door and waved goodbye to her old and new friends. Goldie, however, insisted that she stay. "Seriously? Why not crash here? There's no reason to go home with a strange driver. Especially if you're not feeling well," she smiled. Goldie felt Libby's forehead to make sure she wasn't feverish. In her high-riding vibe, Goldie was especially solicitous. "We'll put you in the Presidential Suite!" She showed Libby to a guestroom and all but tucked her into bed. "There's towels in the closet and soap and tooth-brushing stuff on the sink." She blew a kiss as she exited. Libby collapsed face-down on the bed. The sheets smelled of lavender and hospitality, and Libby dozed. She half-dreamed of bowling with pink Pocky pins.

Care for her mission, alas, kept her from slipping fully into slumber. She threw her leg out from under the comforter, then sat up, then rose, then paced. A little bit after 3:00 AM, Libby emerged from the guestroom and told the few people still awake that she wanted to look at the moon. It was supposed to be full, she said. It wasn't as good an excuse as nipping outside for a cigarette, but Libby didn't smoke. Of course, Libby needn't have worried about her pretext for slipping out. None of the night-owls (a group that did not include Goldie, who'd by then retired) offered to come with her or even looked away from the television screen, where a psychedelic image of the moon now bounced within the frame. No one, therefore, looked askance or took notice at all. Libby thus passed effectively unobserved, even as she stepped over people on her way to the door. She fished her sandals from the pile of footwear in the foyer, but as she left the house, she realized that she'd left her summer cardigan inside—oh well, she'd have to come back for it; there was only one item she needed for the present. She took her phone and went out through the rear gate. Libby was sweating. It was a muggy evening. She looked up. No moon of any kind was visible. *Right*, she remembered, *my phone*. The screen of the diminutive fat lady's Samsung cast the brightest light as it bathed her face in an incandescent orange glow. *Look under contacts.*

Libby called Max-Norm Aire-Girotua, who arrived in half an hour. He'd been sleeping just fine yet bounded out of bed to answer the phone fully awake. He lived only ten minutes away, in Lutherville, but he'd spent time obsessing over the most appropriate aftershave for the occasion. There was not much traffic at that hour. His electric car was silent, as it pulled up. Libby had been waiting for it, though, and knew it was his. He flashed its headlights once. *Okay, I've done my part; I really hope they can work things out.* Libby made a simple hand signal to Aire-Girotua and then returned to her own home via MTA safety shuttle. (The shuttle had initially served only the TU campus, but its coverage was expanded to incorporate all of Towson, when the school bought the suburb.) She walked a few blocks away before hailing it. She missed her cardigan in the air-conditioned chill. She was the only passenger aboard. Traffic was beginning to pick up, as dawn approached. She smiled at the police android on duty, and he/she/it detected no anomaly. Evidently, his/her/its cold sweat sensor was on the fritz.

Sometime after 4:00 AM, Max-Norm Aire-Girotua crept into the house. (He'd spent a few extra minutes in his car attending to his coiffure.) The lunar screensaver illuminated his way. It had done its hypnotic work. All the partyers were now asleep, and Aire-Girotua picked his way to the master bedroom, where he slipped through the open doorway. His senses were heightened. Though he reeked of his own Dior Sauvage, Max-Norm could still detect Goldie's natural scent, which had been implanted in his mind at his first encounter with her, had fortified itself there during his earlier tussle with her, and which now, after her Tappahannock tryst, savored even more sweetly of sex. Max-Norm was now as obsessed as any being was capable of being.

With a knife, he poked through the canopy of the four-poster sleeping platform, and Goldie jumped out. She's been awake but too preoccupied to notice his approach. Evidently, she'd been masturbating. (The effect of her exertions on Max-Norm can only be imagined.) She didn't scream, as though the visit was long expected. She wasn't the least bit sluggish. She was wearing her black Nike Ninja pajamas, and she was ready for action. Max-Norm was surprised. Goldie wrested Aire-Girotua's knife away from him and held him off with it. It was a Fairbairn-Sykes (a.k.a. British commando) knife. When he tried to get it back, she sliced open the back of his hand. Goldie briefly held the initiative. She forced her attacker out of the bedroom and down the hall to the living room, but there he turned on her. He watched a lot of MMA on TV and tried to put some of his education into practice. He kept away from Goldie's slashing blade and sought to improvise for a weapon. Anything cudgel-like would do. Aire-Girotua snatched up the Wii controller and began chasing Goldie around the house. He swung it widely. The bowling game came back on, and the ball jumped into the next lane. He swung it again, with gusto, and the pins went flying. Lamps and serving tables were upset in the scuffle. The lady of the house did not spite the growing wreckage; in fact, she contributed to it. Goldie threw a terracotta statuette of Francis Bacon's Pope Innocent X at Max-Norm, but it missed him and shattered against the mantelpiece. By now, the noise level was surpassing that of the average get-together, and the groggy partiers began to stir. A guest, a caterer named Tinka Klein, was awakened by the racket and started screaming. "We're not giving you any money!" she cried, in Max-Norm's general direction. She kicked wildly to escape from her sleeping bag. Then she started prancing around in random directions, only vaguely aware of what was going on. Others were starting up too. Max-Norm and Goldie continued to melee among them, and chaos reigned. Tinka Klein and an oud player named Ashurbanipal, both naked and dreadlocked to the pubes, leapt back and forth between the modules of Goldie's Italian leather sofa, trying to avoid collateral damage. However, they couldn't remain clear of the violence. Aire-Girotua dealt Ms. Klein a blow on her forehead, and she fell over frontwards. She thrashed around for a few seconds but never got up. Ashurbanipal tripped over a zabuton meditation cushion, sailed through the air, and flopped with a crash through a glass coffee table. Endeavoring to extricate himself from the stainless-steel frame, he lacerated ev-

ery inch of his body with the broken shards and began bleeding pro-
fusely. The remaining occupants of the living room scurried out the
door. In the yard, they were dive-bombed by an angry mockingbird
whose chicks had been eaten by Goldie's cat, and so without tarry-
ing there, they fled in different directions through the neighborhood.
None thought to call the police.

Back inside, the battle wore on. Aire-Girotua continued chasing
Goldie, until all the furniture was wrecked. Max-Norm found pur-
suit difficult through the debris. He growled every time he had to
kick some piece of detritus out of his way. These encounters with
ruined bits of décor where taking a toll on his feet and shins. His
quarry never uttered a single protest. Goldie wouldn't give him the
satisfaction. She was faster but had no place to go, for Max-Norm
was careful to keep himself between Goldie and the door. He batted
away whatever lamp, picture frame, vase, or fat Buddha she threw at
him.

Finally, he caught up with her in the bedroom again. She'd hoped
to find more throwable objects therein, but everything on hand was
soft and cushiony, and so she launched the commando knife at him,
which he dodged, leaving her disarmed. The aromatherapy machine
released a puff of pineapple, just as Goldie realized that Max-Norm
had her trapped. The Juckman princess was defiant to the end. She
turned on him with blazing eyes, but his arm was already descend-
ing. Raising her arms to protect herself would have been undigni-
fied. "You dickless . . ." she began to curse, but Max-Norm landed
his blow on the top of her head, cutting her short. Goldie slowly sank
to a sitting position, and as Max-Norm struck again and again, came
to lay on her side with her back to him. He beat her to death with
the Wii remote. Its "high-impact plastic" construction took on new

meaning. With each bruising blow, the fatal wand registered a gutter ball on the screen in the living room. When ten frames were completed, it started a new game. It was a heavy-duty model that he'd recommended to the Juckman-Schwartzenburgs in happier times. It was probably a bit beyond warranty, but apparently it didn't matter. Max-Norm regarded it with a "Hmm," impressed with its durability. Then he placed it carefully on the nightstand and took in what he'd done.

Goldie's kneecaps were broken, and her head was smashed. Max-Norm remembered the staccato sound his beating had produced. Blood ran in intersecting rivulets down one side of her face from her crown. It was impossibly red, pulsating and gushing, out of place, inhuman, a definite intrusion upon her face. Her defiant expression, however, remained fixed. Her eyes, too, were still open, wide and white with her final scornful glare. It ruined everything for Max-Norm. He lost the staring match with the dead Goldie, and the room seemed to go dark as he turned away. Retrieving his knife, Aire-Girotua slashed Goldie's body from her stomach on down. He grunted like a prehistoric primate. *That'll teach her*, he flared his nostrils; but he was embarrassed to note his teeth chattering and his hands shaking. He wondered what to do next. As he'd long imagined the scene, he was supposed to snarl "whore!" at Goldie's corpse, but in the confusion, he forgot. (It will be recalled that during the earlier attempt on Goldie's life, the help-desk thugs had similarly forgotten to yell "bitch!") Finally, he looked up from his handiwork. He had no idea what time it was but figured he'd better make his getaway. The sun was preparing to rise before Aire-Girotua left. He felt he had to ritualize his departure in some way, but he could only think of one thing to do. He returned the Wii controller to its wicker basket before exiting. That act seemed to convey the necessary finality, but by the time he reached his car, he was waxing sentimental again, and so he reentered the house to take a final look around. Thin rays of morning-light were drifting through the Venetian blinds. They made everything look purple. The rooms were silent, as Alva Noto and Ryuchi Sakamoto's *Vrioon* had long since ended and Alexa had been given no further requests. Ashurbanipal was alive but was keeping still for his own good, to prevent further cuts from the broken glass and for fear of eliciting a beating from Max-Norm. All of Goldie's precious jewelry was scattered about. The collection included Schloss and Juckman heirlooms from as far back as the mid-twentieth century. Some of Cyrus Schumacher's postcards littered the floor as well. Many of these were valuable as novelties. A nude oil painting of Goldie, askew but intact on its hook, looked down on its lifeless model. No one would be making any more of those, of course. The combined lot would have fetched a fortune, but the man who left the estate *in situ* had come on a different sort of business. He was no scavenger. Aire-Girotua took none of it. In quitting the scene as it was, he became its curator. He left Goldie Juckman's safe house as a museum of wasted fortune worthy of the Smithsonian. Its centerpiece was the dead Goldie herself. Outside, the first birds of dawn were beginning to sing. Many now gathered in the forest of feeders that had been placed by Goldie in her usual enthusiasm. Among them were catbirds, mournfully mewing.

Ashurbanipal was reported wandering on Joppa Road around noontime and was taken to hospital unable to account for himself, and the folks who had witnessed the assault thought that they'd only hallucinated it while tripping and thus never did get around to speaking to the police about it; but later in the evening after the fatal morning, the mail drone was finally making its deliveries and, finding the door open, went inside to get Goldie's signature for a package of mango-flavored sexual lubricant and discovered the horrific scene. On the next day, the news spread. Soon it was flashing on every headline feed. The Juckmans had spawned another horror. There was no one commenting online about the case who did not suspect another inside job. Revulsion rose through town with the sickening, hazy sun. People also grieved for the dazzling Goldie and for the unfortunate Tinka Klein, who'd died not long after hitting the floor. The ill tidings reached Velvet Valley Way before the police could bring it. All of the Juckmans were advised right off the bat that they were persons of interest.

Micah and his siblings went to have a look at the scene of the crime. Police officers, both human and android, monitored their behavior. Whether estranged or in cahoots, the various Juckmans met awkwardly in the street outside. They refrained from mentioning the lawsuit between Jeremy and Micah (which was now as dead as Goldie herself and soon to be withdrawn) and in fact conversed very little. "Why Joppa Road?" was the only thing any of them managed to say, as they marched slowly up the walkway. (Towson didn't seem like a fitting place for a Juckman.) The police let them in, one by one. Most of the living room was roped off, giving the visitors only a limited space through which to pass. They were all stunned at what they saw and became unable to speak. (Again, they were already scarcely speaking to each other; but upon beholding the disaster area, they even stopped talking into their phones.) Missy and Zoey were the most impassive of the group. Detectives interpreted their woodenness as repressed female hysteria, as per their programming. Jeremy cried. His wife, Chloe, called him outside and then led him away from the house. His lawyer, also present, kept him from saying any-thing to his older brother. Jeremy and Chloe (and lawyer) got back in their cars and drove away without a word, and most of the other sib-lings also left after only a cursory inspection. Only Micah entered Goldie's bedroom and paid his respects to his dead sister. Micah breathed deeply. Goldie's body had been removed, but the sight of her effects strewn everywhere was overpowering. All of them, of course, were laden with her personality and essence—maybe they *were* her personality and essence—but no, he struggled to realize, she was gone. Forgetting the need to keep his fingerprints to him-self, he grabbed hold of the doorframe for support. *I wonder if she ever grabbed this doorframe for support*, he reflected. Blinking, he strug-gled to keep his vision clear, as he took in the scene. Micah ignored the police android's "Okay, that's enough" and continued his rumi-nations.

He got a close look at the mess. Some of it featured him. There were a few of the old society pictures of him with Goldie, and Micah saw that they'd been folded, as though she (or Bonnie) had kept them in her wallet in the pre-smartphone era. Even the newer items trig-gered old feelings. The nude portrait he'd never seen, and he went into a trance before it. He hated that it was aslant and bent himself di-agonally to be in the same plane. Something like an electrical charge began flowing through the lower part of his torso and he became dizzy. Finally he stood up straight and released the doorframe. He gasped and left. The glare of the outside hurt his eyes. He rubbed his temples as he sat in his car and didn't know where to go. The police recorded it all.

Bonnie Juckman remained in bed and stayed away from Towson that day and for the rest of her life. She never recovered from the loss of her Marigold. Soon, she joined The Ambassador in his mausoleum in Arlington (the Arlington Cemetery of Chizuk, to be precise).

The law belatedly went to work.

Morgan Schwartzenberg, who had not tarried at Goldie's place on the night of the crime, came to doubt that Libby Levin-Khan's appearance on the fatal evening had been a coincidence and reported her to the police. It was time for him to make a positive difference. *Maybe now I can finally do well by Goldie*, he told himself, although the phrase *too little too late* also resounded in his mind. Ultimately, *better late than never* became his guiding principle.

It was a sultry late-summer day when Morgan came to register his suspicious at the Towson Precinct police barracks. It was almost a month since the Joppa Road assault. The file on Goldie's (and Tinka's) murder was still open. The problem remained a lack of reliable witnesses. The investigating detective was Radius Jacobs, a Baltimore native who'd worked his way through UMBC. The Juckman-Klein case was his first big break. Owing to Goldie's status, the police were under pressure to make a quick arrest. Jacobs, however, couldn't afford to be sloppy and so proceeded very methodically. Though speculation about the case was easy, Detective Jacobs knew enough about elite families—the police called them "muckymucks," reviving an old-fashioned term that was suitable for colorful variation—to focus his investigation on the Juckmans' extensive retinue. Muckymucks couldn't do anything without help. Someone among the lackeys was bound to reveal something pertinent. Such people were frequently disgruntled and often a little slow. By means of questioning household service providers, he was beginning to form a picture of the conspiracy. It would have to involve someone akin to a fixer or perhaps someone from the motor pool. Max-Norm Aire-Girotua was an obvious bad egg, but it was best to wait a bit before pouncing on him, pending the clarification of details. Jacobs kept him watched, of course. Then came Morgan's revelation, which gave Jacobs his first solid lead. Libby Levin-Khan hung out with the Juckmans regularly, of course, but she was the first known individual to be placed at the scene (besides Morgan himself, who hadn't remained there and who was considered a spent force when it came to murder conspiracies). The day after Morgan's visit, Detective Jacobs announced that Libby Levin-Khan was a person of interest and began questioning her in a series of afternoon sessions at the barracks. Libby's lawyer was present, naturally, and Micah Juckman coached her between interviews.

Micah sought to dissuade Libby from confessing anything to the authorities. He was, as can be imagined, exhaustive in argument. Indeed, he explained to her, there was nothing to confess, since all she'd done was to help Goldie's concerned family get in touch with her. What happened after that was tragic but unrelated; even so, it would be best to tell the police as little as possible, lest they jump to conclusions. Over the course of three meetings at the Beth El synagogue, which could not be surveilled, Micah calmed Libby's conscience-plagued nerves. In spite of the cantor crooning "Deliver me, O Lord, from lying lips, from a deceitful tongue," Libby was won over once more by Micah's supposed cogency. Exuding his trusted brand of contagious confidence, Micah was quite upbeat. His logic was plausible if a bit ironic. Since the Juckman family was so despised, he assured her, it was unlikely that Detective Jacobs would labor overmuch to seek justice on its behalf. Besides, Jacobs was probably as corrupt as everyone else and unlikely to have any interest in

the case beyond exploiting it. "He'd rather sell the rights to Holly-
wood for a juicy crime story," he pat her shoulder. "If the plot is
full of 'unanswered questions,' so much the better for him." Micah
smiled when he employed this argument. "We're in the clear, as long
as we keep our cool. Just relax," he smarmed. Libby did.

Micah also endeavored to plant doubt in Jacobs' mind. In no wise
intimidated by a mere policeman, he was even more cocky than he
usually was. *Time for a little "These aren't the droids you're looking for,"*
he chuckled. *First I razzle; then I dazzle.* He visited the Towson barracks several times, ostensibly to keep abreast of the investigation,
but he occasionally offered Jacobs free advice. Jacobs took careful
note of everything Micah said. Some of his remarks were intended
to put Detective Jacobs on the defensive. They were appeals to Jacobs' bureaucratic survival instinct. During one conversation, Micah
insinuated that the detective was himself courting investigation for
tolerating Goldie's notorious lewdness on his turf. "How long has
my family been in the news? I mean, think about it: All that sleaze
and the cops didn't know?" Micah whistled. As was the case in his
coaching of Libby, Micah was assuming that the toxicity of his own
name would keep do-gooders at bay.

Muckymucks indeed, Jacobs thought to himself, as he nodded. *Keep
threatening me, punk.*

Got him on the ropes now, exulted Micah inwardly. His meetings
with Jacobs made him feel that he was in the driver's seat.

At this point, however, Max-Norm Aire-Girotua was arrested.
The police had given him a wide berth, confident that the stink
of things would lead to him sooner or later, and now it was time
to talk to him. Detective Jacobs had cross-referenced enough of
Libby's answers to place the bad egg in the center of the ring. No

one was surprised by Max-Norm's arrest more than the overconfi-dent Micah. In fact, Micah had just wrapped up one of his courtesy calls and was leaving the building when Aire-Girotua was brought in. Micah had been beaming, but his soaring spirits now collapsed. *Ooops*, Micah rounded his lips, as Max-Norm was whisked past him and taken to an interrogation room. The evidence against him, con-sisting mostly of Libby Levin-Khan's statements but also of her phone records—including one particularly suspicious call early one ill-starred morning—was put before him, and it was unanswerable. He confessed to the murder of Goldie Juckman. A document was written out for him, and he signed it. His face was emotionless, but his mind was racing with calculation. Having no hope of retaining his liberty, he could still fight for his life, and his best chance was to divert the bulk of the blame to others. Denial, he knew, would do him no good. Rather, he would be the model of cooperation. It would probably count in his favor if he came clean. And so, come clean he did, omitting none of the details.

Aire-Girotua insisted, though, that he had been unwilling to commit the deed and had only been pressured to join the conspir-acy by Libby Levin-Khan, who'd sworn to him that "This is what The Ambassador's son wants. Goldie's been so mean to him, and she's out of control. We have to do it for Micah. There's only so much a man can take." He remembered her words precisely, he said. "She was a real company girl. 'The Ambassador's son will provide cover for us. Micah's so wonderful.' She was all about 'The Ambas-sador's son.' What a ditz." The social media consultant's only play, he realized, was to give the police bigger fish to fry. It would be easy, Max-Norm reasoned, to get both the police and the public to swallow the story of how the naïve girl was used by the spoiled rich kid. His instincts were sound, for the whole city, the whole country, wanted to see a muckymuck face justice. The part about the naïve girl was a side order of red meat.

According to Aire-Girotua, he'd received three thousand dollars directly from Micah, supplemented by about fifteen hundred via Libby Levin-Khan, as an added inducement. "You know the drill. Just follow the money," he told the police, as though they needed his advice. Still, he was playing his part well. Aire-Girotua offered to produce his bank records, which, of course, the police had already obtained. Max-Norm knew that the money trail was a bum steer, for Micah's crew had worked with cash. In fact, it was personal testimony, rather than any financial transaction, that was shining the brightest light on the conspiracy; but in any case, it was clear that both Libby and Micah were deeply involved. Detective Jacobs decided to "climb the tree" and interrogate the one with the lower social status first.

Thereupon, orders were given to arrest Libby Levin-Khan, who was staying in Micah's house. The idea of her lodging there had come from Micah, who promised her the use of his personal masseuse and related pampering but who really just wanted to keep tabs on her. It was on a Sunday morning that Baltimore's finest went to bring her in. The operation was low-key. Anticipating no resistance, the police sent only one cruiser to Federal Hill, and only one officer was needed to walk Libby to it. A larger police commitment would have alerted the press, and images of little Libby being arrested by ten cops would have looked bad. Libby grasped that she was in real trouble only now, as she was led in handcuffs from Micah's townhouse. Alas, it was not the sanctuary she'd been led to believe it was. She'd sought refuge there, thinking that The Ambassador's son would protect her. The spa treatment he'd extended was a further demonstration of his supportiveness. Even though Micah spent most of his time in the hottub, preoccupied with a new crop of groupies, Libby still believed he had her back. (Of course, only the masseuse had her back; Micah had her "wrapped," as the expression goes.) She was a faithful Juckman camp-follower until the end—or nearly to the end, for when she saw that all was lost, she endeavored, as Max-Norm Aire-Girotua had before her, to shift the blame to her supposed protector.

Desperation did its work. Self-interest expelled blind trust with a vengeance. The "fat lady" started singing before she reached the police car. As Libby was escorted out, she insisted that it was Micah who had urged him, via Zoey, to commit the crime. Like all Americans, Libby had pre-acknowledged her Miranda rights on her last tax return, but her concern now was only for Micah's wrongs. She must have incriminated Micah a hundred times that day—calling him always "Micah," never "The Ambassador's son"—in the police car and at the station. She spared no detail that she could recall. She made no attempt to plead ignorance that a crime had been in the working, which, she knew, was an excuse that had only convinced herself. "They played me like a Fender Strativarius [sic]. How could I have been so blind," was as close as she came to an attempt to evade guilt. As long as the police accepted that others were guiltier than she was, she would have said anything. As for the money, it had all been paid by Micah himself, she swore. " 'You deserve it,' he said. All for my 'service to the family'—what a bunch of bullshit. It makes me sick that I fell for it." While on the subject of money, it was Libby's husband, Rusty Khan, who bailed her out of jail. (Libby was not deemed a flight risk, although drones were programmed to follow her even to the toilet.) Had Micah shown up to bail her out (which he did not), Libby would have sent him away. Naturally, everything she said that day was recorded, giving police officers and computers enough material to keep them busy for days.

At length, Detective Jacobs came to grasp the key facts: that Micah Juckman was the chief plotter, Libby Levin-Khan the accessory, and Max-Norm Aire-Girotua the murderer. They became known to beat reporters as "the Captain and Schlemiels." Jacobs knew also of Missy's and Zoey's participation, but direct evidence against the sisters was scant, for they'd been involved mostly in the planning of Libby's Annapolis expedition, which never occurred. Three was a good number anyway. Baltimore County district attorney Allison R. Rhimer moved quickly to produce the indictments. Her department took great care to prevent leaks, so keenly were they awaited. They flashed on phone screens across the nation, as soon as they were unsealed. The details were predictable but complicated. Micah was charged as a younger brother in the murder of his older sister, Libby as the wife of an employee in the murder of her husband's employer's sister, and Max-Norm Aire-Girotua as a former employee in the murder of his former employer's wife. Tinka Klein was also listed as a victim, in the capacity of personal friend of the principal murderer's older sister, etc. The clerk who read the indictments barely got them all out in one breath. He employed a series of charts to show how all involved were related.

The meticulous consideration of social roles in legal proceedings was characteristic of the post-individualist jurisprudence of the late republic, which held that defendants be charged, verdicts rendered, and punishments moderated, according to their relation to the victim; but in the case of *Maryland v. Juckman et al.*, the latter ideal—that of nuanced sentencing—was unrealized. Family and professional relations might have mattered in the adjudication of the myriad minor diddles and swindles that preoccupied legal minds at the time, but not in this instance. It was a capital murder case, after all. Furthermore, the social importance of the chief victim trumped everything—even the fact that poor Libby Levin-Khan had cooperated with the investigation—and at the ensuing secret trial, the three defendants were dealt with uniformly and harshly. All three were sentenced to death by slow dismemberment. No appeal was possible. The verdict surprised no one. It was plausibly rumored to be political. The punishment was handed out by Judge Illrhison Ramer, a well-known FOKK, who acted under direct instruction from Director Kong to avenge Goldie's death. Judge Ramer did not need to be told twice, and his verdict followed Kong's wishes to the letter. It was Kong, incidentally, who had dissuaded prosecutors from bringing even secondary charges against Missy and Zoey, out of a desire to minimize damage to the Juckman family. Micah, however, stank to high heaven, and not even the all-powerful eunuch would stoop to help him—yet other angels protected Micah.

The sentences were only carried out in the cases of Libby Levin-Khan and Maxwell Norman Aire-Girotua. The DOE came a mere week after the verdict (and it would have come earlier, but Labor Day weekend complicated scheduling). Libby was stoic; Max-Norm, still pretending that others were guiltier than he, glared at Libby. Otherwise, he made no fuss. They were disposed of in the same public execution park on State Circle in Annapolis where Arnold Kiester had met his fate some years earlier. The sky was cloudless, and the business commenced just as the sun was clearing the State House cupola. (By this time, the Justice Channel was up and running, and Libby's and Max-Norm's thousand cuts, padded with commercial breaks, worked out to almost three hours of high-revenue airtime.) Let us say no more about that.

One month later, Missy Juckman, who was never charged, went into a fit and jumped off the balcony of her inner harbor condominium. She'd texted no one that day. No one had been with her. She'd switched off all devices that would have left clues as to her movements or activities— except her gaming console. She had been playing Wii bowling all that morning and had just scored 300 before suffering her attack. She didn't remain agitated for long; she simply threw the controller against the wall and bolted toward the sunlight. Apparently, she wanted to go out on a high note. (Her perfect game remained listed in her chatroom's record of achievements for weeks.) People said that she was haunted by Goldie's ghost. Those holding this view maintained that Missy often talked, in the weeks since Goldie's death, as though she were on the phone, although she wore no earpiece and often used the word "sis." Others speculated that she had always envied Goldie and wanted to be just like her dead sister. The fact that Cyrus Schumacher had started pursuing her romantically did not help matters. Medical examiners determined that she was dead before she hit the ground. There was no funeral.

So how had Micah cheated the Reaper? Though conspiracy theorists had a field day with his evasion of justice, it was really just a fluke. Micah Juckman escaped from prison a few days after his sentence was announced. It was indeed a scandal. All suspected an inside job. The FOKK faction, however, could not have had a hand in it, for King Kong himself, resolved at the outset to do nothing for Micah and now embarrassed at the incompetence of the prison authorities, pledged all the resources of the FBI to bring Micah back in. The penitentiary system was turned upside down in search of anyone who might have helped him abscond, but the truth was that his flight occurred during a mandatory evaluation by a child psychiatrist at an unsecured facility. It was a standard procedure, designed to determine mental competence for execution. The good doctor decided to play a game with Micah called "Run Away From Mommy." Achieving transference for the first time despite decades of therapy, Micah toddled with crying eyes, runny nose, and flailing arms through the main gate; and although the state's entire law enforcement network—then undergoing an ill-timed upgrade of operating platform from GoatRope to Fiasco—failed to track him down, no other human being helped Micah escape.

While a fugitive, Micah was indeed protected and assisted by his father's many protégés, now serving in important positions all over the country, who remembered The Ambassador fondly from his long career in ED and also from the online online education seminar he'd taught at Hopkins for many years. (The program secured The Ambassador's fame. Indeed, The Ambassador's online online education seminar kept running for years after his death. Some of its graduates never realized The Ambassador was dead.) These once-young men and women, when shaking The Ambassador's hand (or viewing his talking head) in bygone days, often remarked (or typed into the chat field) that they were "eternally grateful" for all he'd done for them and wished that they could provide comparable service for him or, failing that, for his family. To be sure, some of the Juckman children were more deserving than others, but owing to the dictates of *il patronato*, the lower Micah, in particular, sank, the more The Ambassador's high-flying "students" considered themselves ready to aid him. Now they had their chance, and they were happy to help. With their access to classified law-enforcement information and also to official transportation and lodging options that preserved anonymity, these friends in high places kept their young favorite one step ahead of the law. Therefore, Micah remained at large and was never brought to justice—not while the republic still lasted, anyway. It was a victory of The Ambassador's old school of political networking over the newer, FOKKish variety, but Micah was pleased with the result in any case. Like America herself, Micah Juckman lived well enough for a few years longer, albeit on borrowed time.

Finally, though, time ran out.

In 2044, Washington was sacked by striking public workers. Government buildings were looted and set ablaze by the BPAs, MPAs, MPPs, MPPLs, DPAs, MIAs, MPHs, and JDs who worked in them. Their uprising was triggered when President Pharaoh Frederick claimed a larger-than-negotiated kickback from the pay raise he'd authorized for them. The worker-bureaucrats united in indignation— "Like our votes aren't kickback enough?"—and the violence became widespread. Soon, all of America's major cities were convulsed by riot, and all of America's contemners saw their chance to drink from the Ohio River or to make a track on the Blue Ridge, in the guise of restoring order. They gathered in Turtle Bay. One by one, they promised to send peacekeepers. Baltimore, especially restive, was the first place to which blue helmets were dispatched.

In 2045, Maryland governor Candice Kennedy surrendered Baltimore to the United Nations. She dissolved the city government via Twitter message, and local self-rule came to an end. Governor Kennedy wasn't the first to hope that Mobtown might become somebody else's problem, yet she was the first for whom the hope could be realized; and when she saw how rapidly the city was pacified by the blue helmets, she ceded to them the entire Old Line State. Maryland's citizens, exhausted by mayhem, put up little resistance. As the Governor explained, "I sincerely believe that membership in a world government is the only way to keep the American dream alive. It's time to think big and to think together. The quaint ideal of independence can no longer deliver." With the status quo so demonstrably rotten, no one opposed her, and her argument prevailed. The new regime made her High Commissioner for Jazz Preservation. It was a good gig. She got a bigger office in New York than her old one in Annapolis, and she was able to roll over her 401(k). Half of her staff positions were reserved for trombonists.

All other governors followed Kennedy's example, the erstwhile United States was placed in UN receivership, and the violence subsided, as the original rioters' salaries and benefits were guaranteed. In a matter of months, all thought of strife, or of sovereignty, was forgotten. The American Mandate appeared well on the way to becoming a restored Eden of prosperity, with two solar-powered cars in every garage and a soybean chicken in every pot. Subsidies from every other nation on the globe were raised to finance it, a small price for their juntas to pay to keep the Yankees quiescent.

Micah Juckman, always in search of political protection, considered that "Candy" Kennedy was now a top official in the new government and that her house in Baltimore's patrician Guilford neighborhood would be a fitting refuge. Though lacking an invitation, he assumed that membership in the old aristocracy would get him in the door. *Surely a Kennedy would sympathize with a Juckman*, he persuaded himself. (*Actually*, said Doubt, *the question is: Would a Guilford Kennedy sympathize with a Velvet Valley Way Juckman?* to which

Opportunity barked back, *She fuckin' better.*) He longed to be back in Baltimore, after a long stretch (the second in his life) of laying low, and the thought of staying, even as a fugitive, in stately Guilford in the heart of town, appealed to his suburban self-consciousness. A neighborhood like Guilford is where he always thought he'd retire, and under the circumstances, he might as well retire now. It was a chance to find safety and to hobnob with good people. *I wonder if they're the kind to hot-tub.*

He thereupon took his mistress, Brandi Alewife—who was the wife of a man named Ballantine Alewife—and showed up with her at the Kennedy mansion, Patchwork Clouds. It was summer again, and the closer Micah and Brandi got to their destination, the more the lawns hissed with crickets. They arrived via an antique (and thus untraceable) Plymouth Volare, introduced themselves through the intercom at the front gate, and asked to be buzzed in. The name Juckman did in fact do the trick. High Commissioner Kennedy greeted them cordially and put them up in a camper in the driveway. She looked in to see how they were getting settled and then "left them to it." She sent them a little basket of instant ramen noodles.

A resurgence of political instability made Micah and Brandi happy to have found safe haven of any kind. At the time, the region was freshly embroiled by resistance to the Security Council resolution that American men be required to adopt the mullet hairstyle. Various models of compliance were permissible—from the Kentucky Waterfall to the Mississippi Mudflap—but compliance of some kind was compulsory. The American Mandate's honeymoon period thus came to a speedy end, cut short by a botched directive. The best brains of Turtle Bay had thought it up. The measure was intended to instill ethnic pride in the newly-captive people and thus make them easier to govern, but it oddly backfired, and the UN was now hard pressed to maintain its authority. Cities that had barely cleaned up from recent disturbances were once again racked by disorder. The mullet edict could not be rescinded without a loss of face, and so the blue helmets were again mobilized. Again, they steered their APCs in the direction of Maryland's biggest city.

High Commissioner Kennedy knew that PLA-RCMP peace-keepers were about to reach Baltimore, and so she ordered her major-domo, Kent Hall, to plant a tree before Patchwork Clouds' main gate, as a signal that refugees would be welcomed and protected. Those with unscheduled hairstyles—or those who failed to don the Prince Valiant wigs that signified provisional acceptance of the rules until natural crops filled in— were liable to be shot on sight, if caught on the street. Although Kennedy never repented of her decision to submit to UN rule, she was shocked by the mullet order and the violence it had unleashed. Now she tried to protect everyone she could. Her fear for people's safety was warranted, for UN personnel were determined to punish all recalcitrance. Old world doctrines such as *schrecklichkeit* were re-embedded in the UN soldiers' MO. They scrupled little about making an example of old Mobtown. In addition to gunning down unmulletted men, the People's Volunteers and the Mounties dynamited the Battle Monument on Calvert Street, simply because it was a symbol of the city. During the crisis, as Baltimore was despoiled by the vengeful peacekeepers, the Kennedy compound did in fact house several hundred people, and they remained unmolested—all except two.

The moon had been around the block a few times since the couple's arrival. It was early autumn. Night was falling ever earlier. A curtain of smoke played over the city, fluttering eerily like death itself, and the curtain was about to fall on the house of Juckman. There was a medieval logic to it. Like the royal lineage of a usurped kingdom, The Ambassador's posterity were likewise marked for destruction. They would even be denied modest lives as "remnant subjects."

Micah Juckman's luck finally ran out. He was the very model of the spoiled brat. He had been born lucky, with all the high cards in his hand, but then he'd overplayed it. He'd gambled it all away without having to. His path, wending deviously through cities, countries, and continents, through privilege, ennui, and insatiable hunger, was destined never to issue from Patchwork Clouds. It was a fitting place for him to have ended up, dependent yet ultimately unprotected. Indeed, he'd have been wise never to issue from his camper, but he and Mrs. Alewife hadn't come to Guilford just to be cooped up in a Winnebago; and so they spent most of their days promenading about High Commissioner Kennedy's prize-winning front lawn. One morning, Micah was stung by a yellow jacket, which he should have taken as a bad omen for the afternoon; but the warning went unheeded, and he and Brandi, after lunching on the customary instant noodles, issued forth again, this time to pay a special visit to the Japanese maples abutting the perimeter fence, which were just beginning to blush (and about which Micah cared nothing, but the lawn, again, was prize-winning, and besides, Brandi wanted to see it). A Chinese soldier who'd been posted to stand guard outside Patchwork Clouds was talking on his smartphone, when its face recognition app tagged Micah automatically. For all Micah's arrogance, he believed himself (or at least his crimes) too insignificant to warrant tracking by any national or super-national intelligence agency; oddly, for someone who owed his fortune to technology, he never realized that the latest 13G gadgets could keep tabs on every jaywalker in the world. Even if Micah had undergone twelve rounds of plastic surgery, the Chinese phone would have been able to incorporate every conceivable reshaping into its profile. Micah's record had only a few days before been uploaded to the Chinese system, and the soldier's phone ran it constantly. It flashed red and opened a pop-up, detailing Micah's crimes.

The soldier glanced it over and realized that he had a notorious fratricide on his hands. None of the American's offenses, furthermore, was highlighted by an asterisk, which would have betokened official indulgence. The informal sanctuary status of Patchwork Clouds had been used to flaunt the mullet order, but if High Commissioner Kennedy were shown to be harboring serious criminals like Micah, then the Security Council would have leverage in any negotiation with Kennedy that might resolve the impasse in its favor; both PLA and RCMP personnel guarding Patchwork Clouds had been briefed accordingly. Barely pausing in his conversation, the soldier looked up at Micah and murmured, "開玩笑." (Brandi assumed that the comrade's remark was intended for his phone. Micah actually smiled at the man, thinking that he was trying to start a conversation. He tried to reply, but his tones were off, and his supposed interlocutor wasn't paying attention anyway.) He performed a quick confirmation, and his phone glowed red again. The color-coded alert was superlative and fatal, authorizing shooting on sight. Thus was rendered the verdict. No appeal was possible whenever a PLA phone app was concerned.

Drawing his polonium gun, the soldier discharged it through the wrought-iron perimeter fence, cooking both Micah Juckman and Brandi Alewife from the inside. We'd like to say, "They never knew what hit them," but we would be lying, for they died in prolonged agony. It was as though they'd gotten the chair without having to sit down. Their executioner kept the radioactive bombardment going through the fence for almost five minutes, which was about three and a half minutes past their last shriek. They dissolved into smoking heaps. Of Brandi, who of course was guilty only of attaching herself to Micah, nothing besides her fake Versace vinyl boots remained identifiable; of Micah, there was nothing left but undifferentiated ash. Their dispatcher then returned to his conversation, which was a dialogue on the inferiority of American McDonald's to the ones in China. He was forced to admit, though, that the Americans made better French fries.

Witnessing Micah's death was the former nutritionist of his second wife, Renée Klugman-Juckman. (We hear your knowing chuckles and can respond only with snark of our own. Yes, why wouldn't a prize like Micah have a second wife, and why wouldn't his second wife have a nutritionist? Doesn't every asshole have a second wife, with a nutritionist?) This second marriage had been most unhappy. Also similarly to Micah's first marriage, his second union had been sundered by death. (Gee, what a fucking surprise that is, too.) It had been arranged very quickly. Micah had married Ms. Klugman after poisoning his first wife, Danielle. Danielle's corpse, as can by now be imagined, was not yet cold. It was Bonnie who had pressured Micah to remarry, saying, "For the man which hath a wife is bound by the law to his wife so long as she liveth; but if the wife be dead, he is loosed from the law of his wife." Back then, Micah still listened to his mother, especially when she used her situational Bible quotation app.

Wife Two was unaware of the fate of Wife One and was pleased to become a member of the then-ascendant Juckman family. Even after hearing whispers about Danielle, she remained sanguine. Ms. Klugman's tragic flaw was a curious admixture of naiveté and ambition; she thought, in the language of a bygone era, that she had made "an advantageous match," and she settled into her new life at Juckman Manor with a patient optimism, as though settling into an elevator. For a brief moment, the elevator seemed to be heading upward. Renée, however, refused to shower with Micah, and so he put her aside, settling his affections instead on Brandi Alewife. Once again, deviant sex—or inordinate prudery—had raised its ugly head. Brandi, already hitched to somebody else, labored under no illusions of marrying upward and was motivated by simple hedonism. Simplicity always worked for Brandi (until the very end, that is). Of course, Micah had plenty of other women besides Brandi, but Mrs. Alewife knew better than to be jealous. (So did Mr. Alewife, for that matter.) Mistresses do tend to be more realistic than wives. Thus the mistress was preserved and the wife doomed. Renée Klugman-Juckman had died of rage. She died, alone, while fuming in the shower. Her busted blood vessel at least saved Micah the trouble of poisoning her. Like many other things, Renée's exit was very convenient for him. (At her funeral, Goldie had been the only Juckman present. A number of society reporters was in attendance as well. Thus did Renée finally benefit from marrying up.)

At the time of her death, Renée had had time to employ only a nutritionist and a selfie-stick extender, and the latter moved on after her passing. Her nutritionist, Sari Gaby, remained loyal to her memory. Her devotion was extraordinary. Sari had begun working for Renée when the latter got married, for it seemed that a Juckman woman should have at least one menial; yet since Renée died while still a newlywed, Sari served her chiefly as mourner. Her loyalty was personal, even intimate. She kept pictures of Renée in her bedroom, office—and shower, for she had consoled Renée there in the aftermath of the latter's rejection by Micah. (The night of Renée's final shower had chanced to be Sari's night off.) She lived quietly enough in later years and never expected to cross paths with Micah again, but the political repression of 2045 became so widespread that it soon threatened even semi-reclusive nutritionists, as UN authorities hunted not only the unmulleted but "essential workers" as well— the latter for "volunteer service" in administrative households. In the case of essential workers, no Prince Valiant wig could offer any protection, and all skilled persons were subject to summary impressment, with the result that thousands left their registered addresses to escape such a fate, hiding wherever they could. Ms. Gaby too had fled from the peacekeepers, and that's why she was at Patchwork Clouds, where she was able to observe Micah's belated execution. Long had she prayed to Themis, the goddess of justice, for Micah's punishment. Justice gave her an unobstructed view. She knew Micah and Brandi were at Patchwork Clouds (Micah never recognized her, of course) and peeped at them occasionally, to nurse her resentment; but she had no idea what would greet her eyes that afternoon. She saw the whole thing happen from the widow's watch on the roof. (Unlike the objects of her hatred, she'd been granted access to the house.) Breathing in the smoke that wafted up from Micah's and Brandi's incinerated corpses, Sari smiled and rubbed her locket, which contained Renée's picture. Renée's picture, programmed to respond to the rubbing, smiled too.

Goldie Juckman's youngest sister, Zoey, hanged herself that same day. (The remainder of the Juckman siblings had scattered and sunk into obscurity, following the pattern of once-prominent people during times of upheaval, and only Zoey's fate is known.) Zoey's final residence was a 33rd Street row-house. It was none too glamorous. The rebel of the family, she had married a guitarist named Jethro Johansen who had always worn a mullet and thus was beaten to death by the mob on suspicion of treason. Just as Sari Gaby witnessed Micah and Brandi's deaths, so Zoey witnessed her husband's, with opposite emotional results. Distraught, she resorted to the ceiling fan. Her body was discovered by a platoon of Mounties who'd come to the house to draft her as Tetris tutor to a Saudi prince. Zoey's two daughters, Athena and Amelia, were enslaved by a PLA colonel, who employed them as his personal "lifeguards" at the Milford Mill Swim Club.

How This Book Was Written

F IRST, I CREATED the basic text by translating into English parts of the Chinese anecdotal source "Yushan yao luan zhi" ("Treachery at Yushan"), by Feng Shu (1593–1645). Here are two sentences from this basic text:

> True to what her cousin had told her, Chief Eunuch Wei Zhongxian was then at the height of his influence. On Tiger Hill, in Suzhou, the Puhui Shrine was being built in his honor.

Next, I transplanted the basic text to contemporary and near-future America, resulting in the **Baltimore text**, named for the city I chose to be the main characters' American hometown (although not all the action takes place there). Here is the Baltimore version of the two sentences shown above:

> True to what her cousin had told her, the current Director of the FBI, a eunuch called King Kong, was then at the height of his influence. In Philadelphia's Fairmount Park, King Kong Coliseum was being built in his honor.

Then, I subjected the Baltimore Text to a process called larding, meaning that I inserted one new sentence between every two sentences already there. Larding is one of the many literary exercises favored by the Oulipo coterie of experimental writers. (See Harry Mathews' *Oulipo Compendium* for a full description of larding.) I larded the Baltimore text a total of three times. After the first round, our two sample sentences were now three, and they looked like this (the inserted sentence is italicized):

> True to what her cousin had told her, the current Director of the FBI, a eunuch called King Kong, was then at the height of his influence. *Eunuchs like King Kong had capitalized on the great demand for their employment in both the private and public sectors, where they reduced the risk of costly sexual harassment lawsuits.* In Philadelphia's Fairmount Park, King Kong Coliseum was being built in his honor.

After the second round of larding, the resulting five-sentence passage (with the inserted sentences italicized) read as follows:

> True to what her cousin had told her, the current Director of the FBI, a eunuch called King Kong, was then at the height of his influence. *He had, in fact, just been named person of the year by Time Magazine.* Eunuchs like King Kong had capitalized on the great demand for their employment in both the private and public sectors, where they reduced the risk of costly sexual harassment lawsuits. *The trendsetter in this regard had been media scion Pharaoh Weinstein, whose self-castration on live MeToo TV had inspired young Kong (then known by his rapist name of Mahatma Montessori) to choose the gelded*

path to power. In Philadelphia's Fairmount Park, King Kong Coliseum was being built in his honor.

With the third round of larding (again highlighted in italics), *RASCAL* assumed its final density, as shown in our sample:

True to what her cousin had told her, the current Director of the FBI, a eunuch called King Kong, was then at the height of his influence. *The name King Kong would later figure prominently in accounts of America's decline, but during his own time he commanded respect and no one deemed his rise improper.* He had, in fact, just been named person of the year by Time Magazine. *His auto-biography,* More Balls Than Most, *sat immobile atop the New York Times bestseller list, where it dominated both the political and inspirational genres.* Eunuchs like King Kong had capitalized on the great demand for their employment in both the private and public sectors, where they reduced the risk of costly sexual harassment lawsuits. (*The final liquidation of the Catholic Church in a class-action settlement served as the wake-up call.*) The trend-setter in this regard had been media scion Pharaoh Weinstein, whose self-castration on live MeToo TV had inspired young Kong (then known by his rapist name of Mahatma Montessori) to choose the gelded path to power. *Kong's career, in a few short presidential administrations, led him to his current commanding position in the Bureau.*

In Philadelphia's Fairmount Park, King Kong Coliseum was being built in his honor.

By the numbers (according to textfixer.com): The Baltimore text contained 371 sentences, which grew into 729, then 1407, and finally 2777, with each round of larding. Between every two sentences of the Baltimore text, there are seven in the completed *RASCAL*.

Stylistically, the hardest thing about larding is that each new sentence will separate two sentences that belong together, so that the effect on the text is damaging. A writer seeking merely to mitigate the damage would labor to make each new sentence a general nullity, so that nothing of substance is interposed between the ideally consecutive sentences of the original. On the other hand, if the writer, accepting the challenge of the experiment, wishes to transform the damage into an improvement, then he must craft each new sentence to contain either amusing embellishment or wholly new material that follows naturally from the previous sentence while leading seamlessly to the following one. The new sentence, therefore, loops off in a (hopefully) interesting direction before returning to the original thread of the text. The Oulipo exercise of larding is like being forced to use an extension cord to plug in a lamp that is already right next to the electrical socket. One can try to hide the extension cord (or in this case seven extension cords), or one can make it artistically pleasing enough, perhaps by tinkering it into a string of Christmas lights, to count as an important part of the overall décor.

Harry Miller is a native of Baltimore and a graduate of Wesleyan University. After a sojourn in Taiwan, he settled into academia and now teaches history at the University of South Alabama. He is the author of *Southern Rain*, a historical novel set in seventeenth-century China. Miller is married with three children.

www.ingramcontent.com/pod-product-compliance
Lightning Source LLC
Chambersburg PA
CBHW060244030726
47493CB00025B/2263